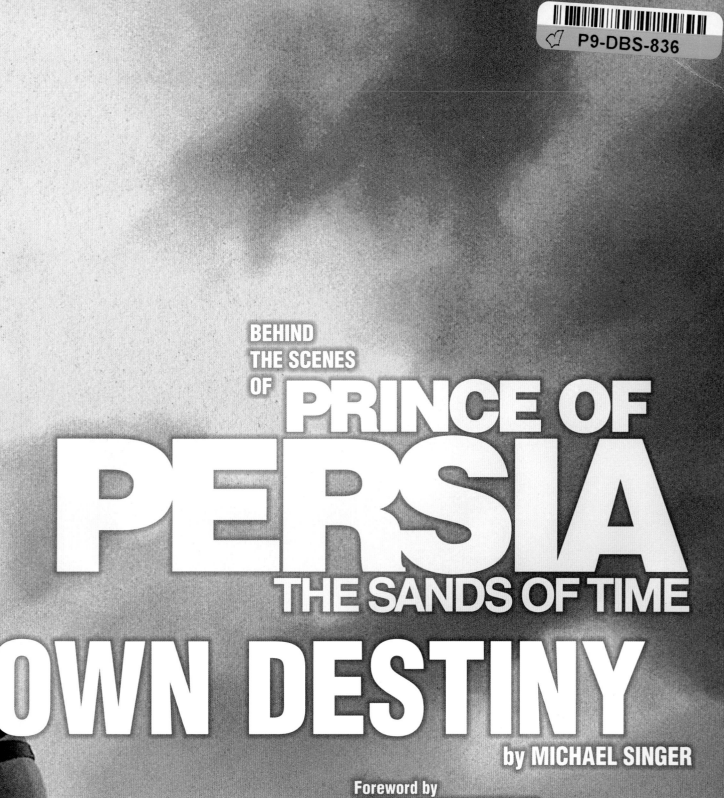

BEHIND
THE SCENES
OF **PRINCE OF**
PERSIA
THE SANDS OF TIME
OWN DESTINY

by **MICHAEL SINGER**

Foreword by
JERRY BRUCKHEIMER

Afterword by
JAKE GYLLENHAAL

A WELCOME BOOK

EDITIONS

NEW YORK

This book's producers would like to thank Jennifer Eastwood,
Jon Rogers, Erik Schmudde, Holly Clark, Braden Wright, Jill
Rapaport, and Erika Nein.

For information address Disney Editions,
114 Fifth Avenue, New York, New York 10011-5690.
Editorial Director: Wendy Lefkon
Assistant Editor: Jessica Ward

Produced by Welcome Enterprises, Inc.
6 West 18th Street, New York, NY 10011
www.welcomebooks.com
Project Director: H. Clark Wakabayashi

Designed by Timothy Shaner and Christopher Measom,
nightanddaydesign.biz

Photographs by Andrew Cooper

Additional photographs in this book
were taken by Jerry Bruckheimer

Page 12: *Morning* by Edmund Dulac, illustration for the
Rubaiyat of Omar Khayyam (1909).
Page 13: *Ali Baba and the Forty Thieves* © 1944 Universal
Pictures. All rights reserved.
Page 19: Edwin Lord Weeks (United States, 1849–1903). *The
Great Mogul and His Court Returning from the Great Mosque
at Delhi, India* (circa 1886). Oil on canvas, 33 5/8 x 54 1/4 inches.
Portland Museum of Art, Maine. Gift of Marion R. Weeks in
memory of Dr. Stephen Homes Weeks, 1918.1
Page 129: *Political Debate in an Opium Den* (1870) by Vasily V.
Vereshchagin. Photo: akg-images, London.

Page 14: Inset images copyright © Jordan Mechner. All
rights reserved. Main image © 2003 Ubisoft Entertainment.
All rights reserved. Based on Prince of Persia® created by
Jordan Mechner. Ubisoft and the Ubisoft logo are trademarks
of Ubisoft Entertainment in the U.S. and/or other countries.
Prince of Persia and Prince of Persia The Sands of Time
are trademarks of Jordan Mechner in the US and/or other
countries used under license by Ubisoft Entertainment.

Artwork by the *Prince of Persia* Art Department:
Kim Frederiksen, Julian Caldow, Peter Popken,
Laurent Beauvallet, and Neil Ross

Prince of Persia: The Sands of Time
Based on the screenplay written by
Doug Miro & Carlo Bernard
From a screen story by Jordan Mechner and Boaz Yakin
Executive Producers Mike Stenson, Chad Oman, John August,
Jordan Mechner, Patrick McCormick, Eric McLeod
Produced by Jerry Bruckheimer
Directed by Mike Newell

Library of Congress Cataloging-in-Publication Data on file.

ISBN 978-1-4231-1754-4

First Edition
1 3 5 7 9 10 8 6 4 2
Printed in China
G559-1249-8-10032

Disney.com/PrinceOfPersia

CONTENTS

FOREWORD
by Jerry Bruckheimer

6

PART ONE
A NEW SUNRISE

9

PART TWO
SHINING STARS

35

PART THREE
SAILING THE
SEA OF SAND

83

AFTERWORD
by Jake Gyllenhaal

174

Beginnings, it is often said, are the toughest part of just about any creative endeavor, including movies. Or, I would say, *especially* movies. A beginning is a time to secure your footing on the right path to making a successful film. The cast and crew are in a getting-to-know-you phase, actors are getting better acquainted with their director, the company is settling on the right style . . . basically, everyone is getting grounded.

At the beginning of our epic production of *Prince of Persia: The Sands of Time* in late July 2008, everybody was *literally* trying to get grounded and secure their footing, since we were filming on a dangerously steep mountainside in the High Atlas range of Morocco at an elevation of more than 8,000 feet! And it wasn't only dialogue or beauty shots that director Mike Newell was filming, but a major action sequence that involved lots of running, jumping, and hell-bent fighting, sixth-century style—a major battle between the hero, Dastan, with his companions, and the lethally dangerous, black-clad Hassansins. Air is a lot thinner at that altitude, and everyone had to very quickly become acclimatized to not only the diminished levels of oxygen, but to the increased levels of adrenaline. That adrenaline would then carry them forward through 100 days of shooting under some of the toughest and most challenging conditions I've ever experienced.

Thankfully, the temperature at that height was relatively cool. Two months later, as we were ending the Moroccan portion of our shoot hundreds of miles to the south of Marrakesh in the amazing Merzouga sand dunes, it was approximately 125 degrees Fahrenheit! Then we were off to England for another three months of shooting, and by the time we wrapped in December it was about 100 degrees colder than that last day in Morocco.

I've always enjoyed adapting the kinds of films I loved watching as a youngster growing up in Detroit, and giving them a swift kick to bring them up to the standards of contemporary moviemaking . . . and beyond. For example, in the mid-1980s, no one was making movies about pilots testing the limits of their courage, since the jet age had dawned in the 1950s. We made *Top Gun*. By the mid-1990s, Cold War suspense movies had expired following the fall of the Soviet Union. We made *Crimson Tide*. Science fiction movies had dropped off in popularity by the late 1990s. We made *Armageddon*. In the first decade of the twentieth century, pirate movies had long since walked the plank as a viable movie genre. We made *Pirates of the Caribbean: The Curse of the Black Pearl*, and then two more in a series that, much to our surprise and joy, became a cultural phenomenon. Everyone said that nobody would be interested in watching a movie about history hunters who use their brains rather than brawn to uncover mysteries about the past. We made *National Treasure* and *National Treasure: Book of Secrets*.

It's been a very long time since the wonderfully magical and colorful world of the ancient Near East has been deemed a suitable backdrop for a major motion picture. Perhaps this is the result of recent history and geopolitics. Although there have been innumerable screen versions of classics like *The Thief of Bagdad*, *Ali Baba and the Forty Thieves*, or Sinbad's seven voyages, they seem to not only be set in a far distant time, but to have been *made* in a far distant time. But in 1989, a very creative and imaginative young man named Jordan Mechner drew on the beauty and mythology of ancient Persia as the foundation of a brand new kind of video game, which he titled Prince of Persia. Just as we had paid homage to the original Disneyland attraction in the Pirates of the Caribbean trilogy while inventing something fresh and new, we were able to use the video game as a springboard for an exciting fantasy adventure film that

would allow us to reinvent an entire genre. We tried to combine the special world that Jordan conjured up in his games with the magnificent history, legend, and lore of ancient Persia. With Mike Newell at the helm as director, Jake Gyllenhaal, Gemma Arterton, Ben Kingsley, Alfred Molina, and thousands of other cast and crew members lending their heroic support throughout the incredibly arduous shoot, *Prince of Persia: The Sands of Time* became a world unto itself.

As the hero Dastan, Jake Gyllenhaal says something toward the end of the film to Princess Tamina, played by Gemma Arterton: "I believe we make our own destiny." This book serves as an invitation behind-the-scenes into the world of a group of people brought together by fate, who each and every day made their own destinies through hard work, craftsmanship, and artistry. Their story was recorded by Michael Singer, someone who was there every day of the shoot, living, eating, sweating, surviving, and having an amazing experience along with the rest of the crew. We'd like to share with you now some of the adventure that was the making of *Prince of Persia: The Sands of Time.*

PART ONE

A New Sunrise

INTRODUCTION
A Persia of the imagination

"We love bringing audiences into new worlds they haven't yet explored," says producer Jerry Bruckheimer, "and ancient Persia is one of the most wonderful of them all. It has such a rich heritage of imagination and fantasy, and we've tried to honor that in *Prince of Persia: The Sands of Time.*"

At a time when European civilization was but a dim gleam on humanity's horizon, mighty Persia was creating great cities and buildings throughout their vast and mighty empire: Persepolis, Baghdad, Susa, Pasargadae, Arg-é Bam, Isfahan. The name Persia has Hellenic roots and is the name by which the country was known in the West until 1935, but the country has always been known to its inhabitants as Iran. Today, the preponderance of historical monuments, ruins, and cultural attractions has led UNESCO to recognize Iran as one of the cradles of civilization, with eight World Heritage Sites within its contemporary borders. Even such landmarks outside of Persia as the Taj Mahal and the Tomb of Humayun in India were strongly influenced by Persian architecture.

It boggles the mind to consider the size and power of the Persian Empire at its height. It stretched from the Euphrates in the west to the Indus River in the east, and from the Caucasus, Caspian, and Aral seas in the north to the Persian Gulf and the Gulf of Oman in the south. In addition to Iran itself, the empire included what are now the modern nations of Azerbaijan, Afghanistan, Pakistan, Turkmenistan, Tajikistan, Uzbekistan, and the eastern parts of Turkey and Iraq and their surrounding regions. Persian architecture, from the soaring ziggurats, lavish palaces, and hanging gardens of antiquity to the magnificent mosques of the Common Era, is almost unprecedented in its fusion of technology, artistry, and spirituality.

One would expect a civilization more than 7,000 years old to have made at least some notable contributions to the world, but with its poets, writers, composers, architects, scientists, doctors, and mathematicians, Persia has poured unimaginable riches into the treasure trove of world culture. The ninth-century Persian mathematician Muhammad ibn Musa-al-Khwarizmi is the father of algebra. Six hundred years before Charles Darwin, a Persian scientist and theologian named Nasir al-Din al-Tusi developed the basic theory of evolution. Persians invented the windmill and created an early form of electrical batteries. In the ninth century, Jabir ibn Hayyan unleashed alchemy from superstition and invented chemistry as we know it today. The man considered the father of optics—Abu Ali al-Hasan ibn al-Haitam, or more simply, Alhazen—was an Arab born in 965 AD in Basra, Iraq, which was then part of the Persian Buyid Empire. And, considering his experiments with lenses, mirrors, refraction, and reflection, he might also be considered the father of cinema, which relies heavily on the principles he was discovering.

Unthinkable is a literary world without the *Rubaiyat of Omar Khayyam*, a collection of nearly 1,000 poems. Khayyam was a scientist with the soul and artistry of a poet, whose contributions to the cultural lexicon included the phrase "a loaf of bread, a jug of wine, and thou"—as sure a recipe for a good life as any other proposed in the 800 or so years since those words were written. Also highly influential were the works of the thirteenth-century mystic Rumi, whose spiritual poetry became hugely popular in the West in the late twentieth century. Two great works of Persian literature significantly influenced Jordan Mechner when he created his Prince of Persia video game: the *Shahnameh*, a massive work written by the great poet Ferdowsi in approximately 1000 AD and considered to be the national epic of Iran; and *One Thousand and One Nights*, a collection of stories dating back to the ninth century that quite brilliantly incorporated ancient Persian, Middle Eastern, and Indian folktales and legends. The stories exist within a frame tale about a queen named Scheherazade, who is at risk of being executed by her murderous husband. In order to forestall her death, she keeps her husband enthralled by telling him one extraordinary story after another.

Throughout the ensuing centuries, parts of the original manuscript of *One Thousand and One Nights* have been reap-

propriated and augmented by numerous editors and embellishers, feeding the imaginations of million of readers—not to mention moviegoers. Several of the stories from the collection—also called *Arabian Nights*—have been recreated in film multiple times as both live-action and animated versions. The most well-known tales are "Aladdin's Wonderful Lamp," "Ali Baba and the Forty Thieves," and "The Seven Voyages of Sinbad." Ironically, none of these stories were in the original *One Thousand and*

ABOVE: Dastan (Jake Gyllenhaal) and Tamina (Gemma Arterton) ride Aksh through the desert, filmed in the stunning Merzouga sand dunes near Erfoud, Morocco; RIGHT: Dastan (Jake Gyllenhaal), Tamina (Gemma Arterton), and Sheikh Amar (Alfred Molina) at the foot of the Alamut Sky Chamber.

One Nights, but were most likely Arabic folktales woven into the collection by early European translators, such as the Frenchman Antoine Galland. The story of Aladdin, of course, was adapted by screenwriters Ted Elliott and Terry Rossio, composer Alan Menken, and lyricist Howard Ashman in the now-classic 1992 Disney animated version. (Elliott and Rossio would later work with Jerry Bruckheimer on the Pirates of the Caribbean trilogy and the two National Treasure films.) The first noted screen version of Aladdin's tale dates back to 1922 and was directed by Oscar-winner Norman Taurog.

However, Ali Baba's tale trumps Aladdin's with regard to cinematic interpretations, having been retold with a camera nearly fifty times since 1902 in countries as diverse as Russia, Hong Kong, Brazil, Japan, France, Italy, and Malaysia. And the exploits of Sinbad were very familiar to anyone growing up from the late 1950s to the late 1970s. Audiences were thrilled by the legendary special effects in genius Ray Harryhausen's *The 7th Voyage of Sinbad, The Golden Voyage of Sinbad*, and *Sinbad and the Eye of the Tiger*. These films were by no means the only screen versions of the exploits of the famed sailor; other film-makers around the world also had a go at the legend, in some thirty-five other films. Numerous other film and television adaptations of Scheherazade's stories have been made, proving that the appeal of the Persian tales is universal and timeless.

This Persia of the imagination, a Persia in which the fantastical finds its way into every aspect of the culture, reveals a civilization with a keen and profound sense of its own magic and mystery. It was this magic and mystery that excited and inspired Jordan Mechner when he was creating his seminal Prince of Persia video game in 1989. Mechner recognized that he could create an alternative world based upon the historical realities of ancient Persia, creating new mythologies about a culture that had created so many of its own fantasies for thousands of years.

OPPOSITE: An atmospheric image by French book illustrator Edmund Dulac for a 1909 edition of the Rubaiyat of Omar Khayyam; *ABOVE: Spanish poster for the 1944 American screen version of* Ali Baba and the Forty Thieves; *BELOW: Concept illustration of the royal city of Nasaf shows how the original structures of Kasbah Ait Ben Haddou were incorporated into the overall design.*

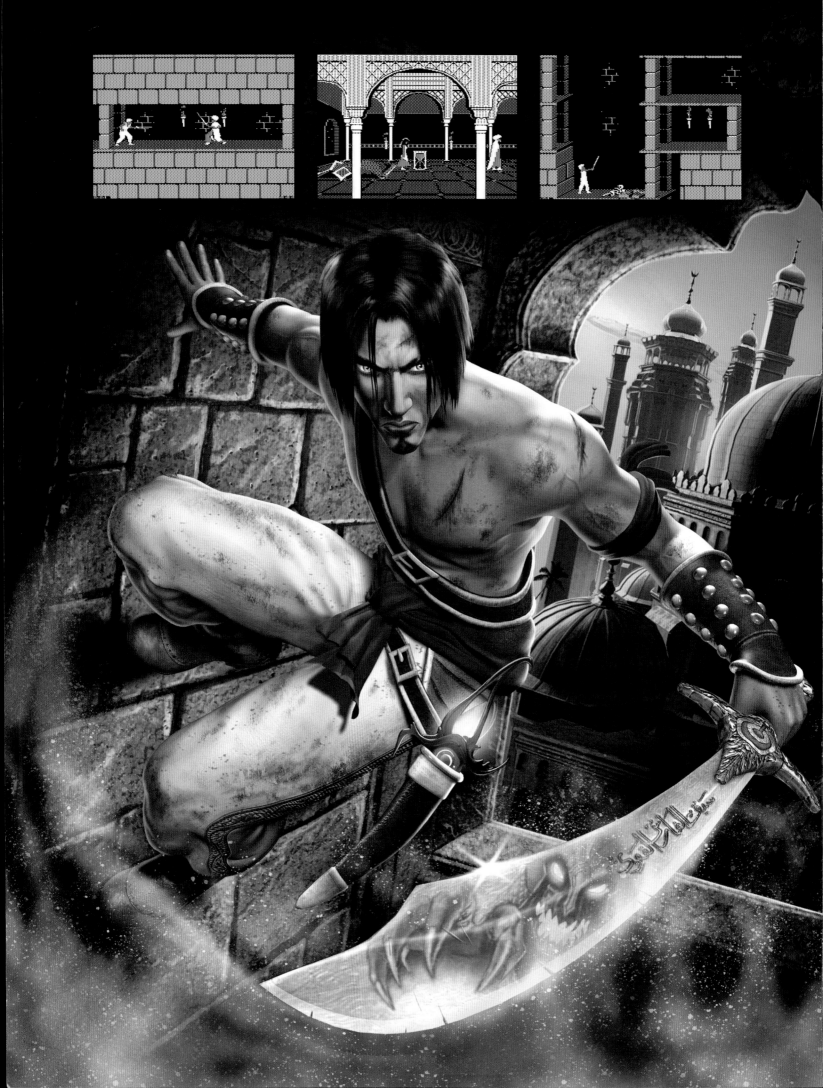

Rising from the Sands

It was 1985, and I was looking for a universe that hadn't yet been done to death in video games," recalled Jordan Mechner while calmly enduring the 115-degree heat in the Fint Oasis outside of the southern Moroccan city of Ouarzazate. He was visiting the set of the film based on his creation and he remarked, "The universe of *One Thousand and One Nights* is such a rich treasure trove of stories and characters, it seemed tailor-made for the kind of swashbuckling action that I wanted to do. It's got really deep roots in world culture, and I think it's something that's sort of in all of our collective unconscious.

"The early days of video games were kind of like the early days of cinema," Mechner explains. "We were looking to previously established genres to find things that worked in this new medium, like sword and sorcery and science fiction. Works like *Arabian Nights* have a resonance that comes from the fact that the world of the East is so mysterious, and we know about it from childhood. No matter what culture you come from, *One Thousand and One Nights* has a kind of fascination. We kind of know about it without really knowing how we know about it, and so the direct inspirations for the first Prince of Persia game were probably both the 1924 and 1940 film versions of *Thief of Bagdad*. With Prince of Persia I also wanted to create a character who would feel like flesh and blood—like if he missed the jump, it would really hurt."

For the protagonist of Prince of Persia, Mechner created a figure who defied gravity with his acrobatic acumen, yet remained governed by the laws of physics and human capability. Mechner was not only creating a character who leapt from one precipice to another; the young video game genius was also taking a giant leap himself, seeking new technologies to bring his world of Prince of Persia to life as fully as possible—little knowing that twenty years later, he would be melting in the Moroccan heat, happily watching his creation make another dramatic leap: from video-game console to the big screen.

"It's mind-boggling to think that a production of this scale started as an eight-bit Apple II computer game," says Mechner, who also served as one of the executive producers for the film. "And, just as the original game was inspired by Hollywood movies like *Thief of Bagdad*, which was inspired by the stories from *Arabian Nights*, perhaps this movie will be an introduction for our younger audiences to the world of *One Thousand and*

One Nights or the *Shahnameh*, the Persian Book of Kings. The wheels keep turning."

ODYSSEY TO THE BIG SCREEN

The screen version of *Prince of Persia: The Sands of Time* was founded not only upon the rock of Mechner's video games, but also on an initial draft of the screenplay which Mechner wrote himself. He had written it several years earlier at the behest of Jerry Bruckheimer Films, when that company first decided that there was an epic movie to be found in Mechner's creation. "I love exploring worlds that haven't been seen on-screen before," says Jerry Bruckheimer, "and the world of the Prince of Persia video game was fascinating. It had a wonderful fantasy aspect about it, and the sands-of-time element introduced in the 2003 game was perfect for the big screen. We felt that we should have elements of the game, but, just as we did with Pirates of the Caribbean, develop our own story, taking off from what was given us. But we think we're being true to Jordan Mechner's vision of the game.

"We tackle epic films, from *Armageddon* to *Pirates of the Caribbean*. And *Prince of Persia: The Sands of Time* falls right in line with those kinds of movies," notes Bruckheimer. "It's got enormous imagination, and enormous scope, and phenomenal action, and takes place in a world that audiences have never seen before."

OPPOSITE: Images from the original Prince of Persia *game (insets) and from the 2003 edition,* Prince of Persia: The Sands of Time; *RIGHT: Jordan Mechner on set in the Big Fint location in Morocco.*

Bruckheimer understood that a video game and a motion picture are two completely different animals. "Video games don't have the time to create in-depth characters," says the producer, "so you embellish and create story, using the game as a guide. It's a challenge to create a film that satisfies the gamers, but not everyone in the audience plays the game. They just want to get themselves lost in an adventure, and that's what we set out to do, taking them on a fantastic journey."

"There was some concern about the stigma attached to previous video games, which had been turned into really bad movies," notes executive producer and Jerry Bruckheimer Films president Mike Stenson. "But we felt that the game-play elements of this movie—particularly the parkour aspect and the fact that we could tell a really classic adventure story—made it unique and lent itself to an epic, *Lawrence of Arabia*-style treatment. Prince of Persia had a lot of mythology and richness to it, and we thought that the time rewind was very cinematic. And also, to some extent, we thought that it could be a great follow-up to the Pirates of the Caribbean movies, another epic that's fun and entertaining, but founded in history."

"Jordan Mechner came in and pitched a story about a young prince who is falsely accused of killing his own father, the king, and has to go on the run," adds executive producer Chad Oman, president of production for Jerry Bruckheimer Films. "That alone felt like a really interesting story, with great action and romance built into it. The ability to do a beautiful epic period piece, com-

bined with the humor of a romantic adventure, really pulled us to it. And we loved the concept from the Sands of Time game of being able to reverse time. The prince is taking a journey of discovery, learning the weight and responsibility of destiny. The game play was amazing, with a lot of fun swordplay and acrobatics. We've tried to stay true to the concept and characters of the game, with the game play inspiring the choreography of our action."

Jordan Mechner embarked on adapting his games for Jerry Bruckheimer Films laying a great foundation for further contributions from other writers. "The overall thrust and basic beats of the story, as well as the characters' names of Dastan and Tamina, came from Jordan," says Mike Stenson. "Jordan has remained involved with the film every step of the way, and has been terrifically helpful and supportive."

"The movie draws on all the games, but it's really an adaptation of The Sands of Time, the first Prince of Persia game that I did with Ubisoft," explains Mechner. "In some ways, The Sands of Time is tailor-made for a movie, because it's not just a series of action set pieces. But the surface similarity between a movie and a video game is deceptive. They're very different media, and the difference is that movies are meant to be watched, and video games are meant to be played. The Sands of Time video-game story was really designed as a playing experience, and the fact that the Prince in the game has no name is great, because he's someone that you, as the player, can project yourself onto.

"But in a movie," Mechner continues, "the hero is someone that we're going to be watching for two hours, and it's someone who has got to be a real human being, with a specific history, family, and name. So in adapting The Sands of Time into a movie, we had to give the Prince a name, and 'Dastan' comes from the *Shahnameh*, the Persian Book of Kings:

> [The Simorgh] went to the youth and said, 'O brave young man, until today I have brought you up as if I were your nurse, and I have taught you speech and the ways of virtue. Now it is time for you to return to your own birthplace. Your father has come searching for you. I have named you Dastan [the trickster], and from now on you will be known by this name.'

A name meaning 'trickster' seemed perfect, because Dastan is an underdog who's a bit mischievous and gets by with his cleverness. The trickster is an archetypal character that goes through both literary and film history."

LEFT: Tamina (Gemma Arterton) and Jerry Bruckheimer on set.

*What appealed to us about the Prince of Persia game was the way in
which it combined historical fiction with fantastic events.*

— screenwriter Doug Miro

Mechner discovered that the word *dastan* had "shadings I wasn't aware of—shadings that make it an even more appropriate name for the prince than I realized. First, several people—including Jake Gyllenhaal, the first day we met—have pointed out to me that dastan is also a Persian word meaning 'story.' According to Wikipedia, a Dastan is a type of Central Asian oral history 'centered on one individual who protects his tribe or his people from an outside invader/enemy.' Hey, just like every video game."

As for naming the princess, Mechner explains, "There's a character in Mozart's opera *The Magic Flute* named Pamina and an old Persian name, Tamino, so I combined those into Tamina, which not only sounds beautiful, but also happens to be another old Persian name."

Following Mechner's initial draft of the screenplay, the development process accelerated. Among the writers taking a crack at the script was Boaz Yakin, who had directed the popular football-based drama *Remember the Titans* for Jerry Bruckheimer Films in 2000.

"Boaz came up with a new mythology for the first part of the script based on the Moses story," explains Mike Stenson, "in which our hero is an adopted child brought into the royal family, never really feels as if he's a part of it, but then grows into his destiny. For the first act, that worked great for us."

Jerry Bruckheimer, Stenson, and Chad Oman then enlisted a pair of young screenwriting partners named Doug Miro and

Carlo Bernard. "They had a great take on the rest of the story," notes Stenson, "ultimately taking the foundation that Jordan gave us, and the core first act that Boaz gave us, and carrying it through the whole movie. Doug and Carlo wrote all the way through production in Morocco and England, with either one or the other, or both, almost always on location."

As is the case with so many other successful partnerships, Miro and Bernard are an amusing study in contrasts, from their heights (Carlo's the tall guy) to their demeanor (Doug is the more loquacious). But as writers, they're quite literally on the same page. "What appealed to us about the Prince of Persia game," Miro explained during a break in filming at Kasbah Taourirte in Ouarzazate, "was the way in which it combined historical fiction with fantastic events. We've always been interested in period movies, and this provided us an opportunity to write an epic with a lot of action and spectacle, which would appeal to a broad audience."

"The visual world of the game was incredible, and that's what really got me excited," adds Bernard. "Jerry encouraged us to be really ambitious with our approach, and I think—and hope—that the project exceeds what people imagine when they think of a movie based on a video game. For us, it was just about trying to tell a fantastic story, which happened to be based on an amazing video game."

"There was always an impetus to add a sort of Shakespearean element to the story," comments Miro, "with characters, emotion, and story. The video game was a great launching point for trying to tell a great tale. The mythology certainly is not what's been in a lot of recent movies. It's dramatic, romantic, and spectacular."

Now it fell to Jerry Bruckheimer, as it had so many times over the course of his forty-year career as one of the most successful producers in motion-picture history, to find the right director to bring the whole, massive enterprise to cinematic life. And for that, he turned his gaze eastward from his Los Angeles base of operations, across the States and the mighty Atlantic.

MIKE NEWELL:
THE MAN FOR THE JOB

On the other side of the pond, one of Great Britain's more distinguished inhabitants was surprised to receive a note from Jerry Bruckheimer asking him if he might be interested in directing the screen version of *Prince of Persia: The Sands of Time*. "I had no idea that Jerry would even know of my existence," exclaims Mike Newell.

Not bloody likely that Jerry Bruckheimer *wouldn't* be aware of Mike Newell. "Mike can do just about any kind of movie," notes the producer, "from *Four Weddings and a Funeral*, which is a dramatic comedy, to *Donnie Brasco*, a hard-edged, gritty

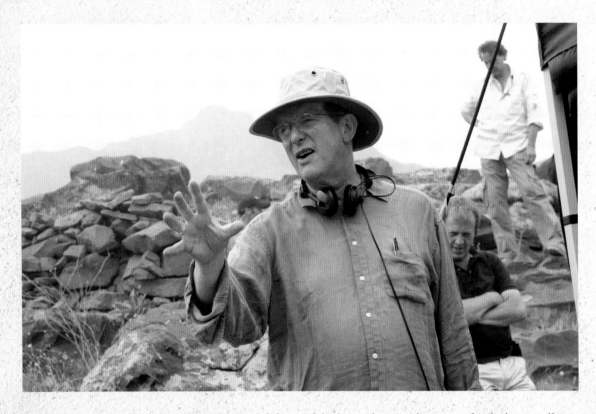

street movie. And then he goes and does *Harry Potter and the Goblet of Fire*, which had just the right blend of adventure and mystical fantasy that we were looking for. Mike has a really wonderful palette that he paints from, and that's very important to us. We want an entertaining film that appeals to a broad audience, but also something special that concentrates on character and story."

Interestingly, one of the lures that Jerry Bruckheimer used to whet Mike Newell's interest in directing *Prince of Persia: The Sands of Time* was a book about Orientalist art filled with gorgeously detailed, color-saturated canvases recording the life and lore of the Middle East. "They were like documentary cameramen," says Newell of the Orientalists. "They went in and painted what they saw with a tremendous kind of romanticism, which was the mind-set of the times in which they lived. So what you see is a highly colored, very romantic, very strange and tempting kind of world."

Orientalist art was a nineteenth-century Western cultural movement that glorified and romanticized the Middle Eastern world. But like any romantics, Orientalist artists were deeply and hopelessly in love with their subjects, and their adoration was reflected in works imbued with creative passion.

Although the Orientalist art style has suffered from neglect for the last several decades, an April 10, 2009, article in the *New York Times* titled "Recapturing the Allure of Orientalist Art" confirms that appreciation of the form is being renewed. Columnist Wendy Moonan wrote, *"Such works have long been considered paternalistic and condescending, a product of European colonialism. Orientalist art, even its masterpieces, was denigrated by critics as lacking in artistic merit. Now opinion is turning. In recent years collectors have embraced the art for its fascinating subject matter and painterly qualities."* The ar-

ticle then points out that most of today's top collectors of Orientalist art are, themselves, Middle Eastern, including Salim Moussa Achi and Egyptian businessman Shafik Gabr. In the *Times* article, Mr. Gabr is quoted as saying of Orientalist artists, *"They were respectful onlookers. Whatever it was they chose to paint, these artists were fascinated by and anxious to record our world, our customs, our architecture, our habits. We owe them a great debt."*

Mike Newell was also drawn to the project by the story's mythical aspects. "What I loved was that it was like a Bible story," notes the director. "It was like Noah and the Ark, going way back to the time before stories were history. It went back to a point when they were myth." Although he wasn't a gamer going into the project, Newell admits, "I got my trusty helpers to score me the Prince of Persia video game, and I became completely hooked. It's a very difficult circle to square, to tell a story that we've developed that will also satisfy the gamers.

"But when you tell people that it's a Jerry Bruckheimer production, and a Walt Disney picture, that seems to satisfy people," continues Newell. "In Britain, we were all brought up on little films. And the more exquisite, the more dark, the more agonized, the more true to our filthy, fallible human natures a film can be—that's a good Brit picture. But later, I got really interested in great big entertainment—one of the reasons I directed *Harry Potter and the Goblet of Fire*. *Prince of Persia: The Sands of Time* is exactly that—great, big entertainment—and I'm very pleased to have it."

ABOVE: Mike Newell directs in Morocco's High Atlas mountains in Oukaimden; RIGHT: A typical example of nineteenth century Orientalist painting, Edwin Lord Weeks' Great Mogul and His Court Returning from the Great Mosque at Delhi, India (detail, ca. 1886).

portrait of a producer

The now-familiar and rather poetic logo of Jerry Bruckheimer Films and Television is an animated image of a
lightning bolt striking a lone, bare tree on the side of a
long stretch of highway.

Jerry Bruckheimer is the man riding that lightning bolt.
The producer (an appellation invariably preceded by the word
mega) is an unabashed all-American in the classic Horatio
Alger mode. The Detroit-born son of German immigrant par-
ents, Bruckheimer graduated from the University of Arizona
and went on to pursue the American dream, first in advertising,
then in motion pictures and television. Along the route, Jerry
Bruckheimer became the most successful producer in film and
television history, with a daunting list of credits that reads like
the popular history of the United States from 1980 onward. Now
approaching the fortieth anniversary of his first big-screen production, Bruckheimer has an impressive résumé. He and Don
Simpson produced *Flashdance, Beverly Hills Cop, Top Gun,
Beverly Hills Cop II, Days of Thunder, Bad Boys, Crimson Tide*,
and *The Rock*. Since the creation of Jerry Bruckheimer Films,
Bruckheimer has produced, among other movies, *Con Air*,

*Armageddon, Enemy of the State, Gone in Sixty Seconds, Coy-
ote Ugly, Pearl Harbor, Black Hawk Down, Bad Boys II, King
Arthur, National Treasure, Déjà Vu, National Treasure: Book of
Secrets, Confessions of a Shopaholic, G-Force, The Sorcerer's
Apprentice*, and, of course, the thunderously successful Pirates
of the Caribbean trilogy. In addition to his audience-pleasing
blockbusters, Bruckheimer has also nurtured films that have
pondered political and social themes with considerable courage
and insight, including *Dangerous Minds, Veronica Guerin*, and
two sports films that were as much about the subject of race in
America as they were about football and basketball respectively:
Remember the Titans and *Glory Road*.

For the small screen, Bruckheimer has produced shows
that consistently garner high ratings, including the three phe-
nomenally successful CSI programs, *The Amazing Race, Without a Trace*, and *Cold Case*.

Such accomplishments do not happen by accident, and the
proof of Jerry Bruckheimer's almost preternatural success is in
the numbers and the honors. Worldwide, his films have earned
well over $15 billion in box-office, video, and recording revenues

(the Pirates of the Caribbean trilogy alone took in almost $2.7 billion internationally). In the 2005–2006 season he had a record-breaking ten series on network television, a feat unprecedented in nearly sixty years of television history. His films—sixteen of which exceeded the $100 million-mark in U.S. box-office receipts—and television programs have been acknowledged by a slew of awards. The full panoply of ego-tickling kudos—Oscars, Emmys, Grammys, Golden Globes, People's Choice Awards, BAFTA Awards, and MTV Awards—have descended upon Jerry Bruckheimer like cherry blossoms in May. Add to that his consistent recognitions on the annual magazine lists of "Most Powerful," "Most Influential," and "New Establishment," year after year.

All very nice, but in the end, what Jerry Bruckheimer is really all about is taking the audience on a journey.

"I always like to say that we're in the transportation business," says Bruckheimer, sitting behind his large, sleek, rectangular desk at the company headquarters in Santa Monica, California—an unmarked red-brick building in a rather gritty industrial neighborhood. His office boasts an impressive collection of classic fountain pens, a full-size suit of Roman armor from *King Arthur*, a painting of a hockey player given to him by daughter Alexandra, and a shelf holding many of the afore-

ABOVE: Co-fight coordinators Thomas Dupont (in Hassansin costume) and Ben Cooke work with Jake Gyllenhaal on a fight sequence filmed in Oukaimden in Morocco's High Atlas mountains; RIGHT: Jerry Bruckheimer talks with Jake Gyllenhaal in the same location.

mentioned honors. "We like to transport people to other places. I think people always want to get taken away from their lives, to get lost in other places and other characters for a couple of hours. That's the way I felt as a kid in Detroit, sneaking off to the movies, and that excitement still hasn't changed a bit."

Perhaps too modestly for a man as comfortable in Armani as he is on a hockey rink, Bruckheimer has always taken a determinedly non-elitist stance when describing himself. Despite being a self-proclaimed "mainstream cheeseburger kind of guy," Jerry Bruckheimer's contributions to popular culture cannot be underestimated. His experience in advertising was a fine educa-

tion for what was to come later, because in making commercials, he essentially created mini-movies that swiftly got the point across in thirty to sixty seconds. Emerging from the advertising world, Bruckheimer then combined a classical storytelling sensibility with a highly innovative, deeply visceral approach in making his motion pictures. Bruckheimer's films were at least partly responsible for rebooting the visual language of mainstream American cinema, starting with *American Gigolo* and *Thief*, which he made in his pre-Don Simpson days. Bruckheimer was one of the first producers to recognize the value of hiring directors of TV commercials and having them apply their flair for striking imagery to the big screen. He went on to reboot television series by bringing a feature-film style to that medium, recognizing that a smaller screen does not necessitate a smaller sensibility.

The "secret" of Bruckheimer's success is deceptively simple: "I just make movies and television series that I want to see." No market research or demographic research necessary for this producer, no wild swings in the dark at wondering who the audience is, because Jerry Bruckheimer *is* the audience. He goes by his instincts (the *Washington Post* once referred to him as "the man with the golden gut"), and, considering the fact that he's a confessed populist, his tastes are often right on par with not only the great American public, but also the even greater international public. Jerry Bruckheimer has become a household name from Tokyo to Texarkana, although the man himself remains quietly enigmatic, rarely inviting scrutiny of the private life that he shares with his wife, best-selling novelist Linda Bruckheimer (*Dreaming Southern*; *The Southern Belles of Honeysuckle Way*). As for the sheer amount of work and effort that goes into keeping so many balls in the air at one time, perhaps it's best explained by an anonymous saying that hangs framed in the photocopy room of Bruckheimer's office building: *"The way you do anything is the way you do everything."* And the way

Jerry Bruckheimer does anything *and* everything is to push it to the absolute limit—and then a little farther.

"He's tireless in his pursuit of trying to make something better," confirms Chad Oman, the president of production for Jerry Bruckheimer Films. "Even if the scene is good and everyone's happy with it, he'll want to go back to the well and see if we can make it better, long after the point where most people are ready to quit on something."

There are few contemporary producers who can honestly inherit the mantle passed down by such past cinematic visionaries as Zanuck, DeMille, Zukor, Goldwyn, Selznick, or, for that matter, Walt Disney—all men who were unafraid to lay it on the line. Like Disney, Bruckheimer has spun his empire of dreams by focusing on the fine art of entertaining millions of people from disparate cultural and economic backgrounds. Like Disney, Bruckheimer has an infallible faith not only in the American dream and its limitless possibilities, but also in the certainty that that dream can, and does, come true. And, like Disney, Bruckheimer has brought a completely independent, maverick spirit into the Hollywood mainstream.

Perhaps it was inevitable, then, that two of Hollywood's most recognizable branded names—Disney and Bruckheimer—would engage in what has proven to be a long and unusually fruitful association, which now dates back nearly fifteen years. "Walt Disney obviously has the strongest brand profile of any studio in the business," notes Jerry Bruckheimer. "The reason I'm there is because they're so good at what they do. They're really great with their marketing and distribution, and of course, have wonderful executives."

The most obvious results of this creative collusion between studio and producer can be seen in the blockbuster Pirates of the Caribbean trilogy. In making the three films, Jerry Bruckheimer and director Gore Verbinski took the seed of the great Disney attraction (the last one in which Walt Disney was personally involved before his death), and cultivated it into an international phenomenon that truly took on a life of its own. "Pirates" has now taken its place in the pantheon of motion-picture greats, with Johnny Depp's portrayal of the magnificently eccentric Captain Jack Sparrow routinely topping the lists of the all-time most popular screen characters.

After completing *Prince of Persia*, Jerry Bruckheimer applied a similar philosophy to another huge-scaled fantasy epic, *The Sorcerer's Apprentice*, which draws inspiration from one of Walt Disney's most beloved projects: the 1940 film *Fantasia*. Elements from the animated feature would be woven into an all-new and highly ambitious film starring Nicolas Cage (in his seventh collaboration with Bruckheimer), rising star Jay Baruchel, newcomer Teresa Palmer, and *Prince of Persia* cast members Alfred Molina and Toby Kebbell. Bruckheimer would

LEFT: Property master David Balfour shows the Dagger of Time to Jerry Bruckheimer and executive producer Chad Oman in Morocco; OPPOSITE: Jake Gyllenhaal finds himself in a precarious position nearly 9,000 feet up in the mountain location of Oukaimden.

also have a familiar face in the director's chair—Jon Turteltaub of *National Treasure* and *National Treasure: Book of Secrets.*

What does such a relentless go-getter do for vacations? "I don't take many of them," he notes with a smile. "When you really love what you do, you don't feel the need to get away." For relaxation, Jerry Bruckheimer takes photographs with a battery of high-tech cameras—often on the sets of his own films—and some of those incisive images have been displayed in exhibitions around the world. "I love photography, and it's been a hobby of mine since I was six years old," he admits. "It allows you to see the world in a special way."

Indeed, Ronald Pickup, who portrays King Sharaman in *Prince of Persia: The Sands of Time*, recalls an amusing anecdote: "Near the end of the first day I was on set in Morocco, there was somebody standing in front of me on the steps of Alamut Palace taking pictures, and I knew that pictures were only supposed to be taken by the unit photographer. I was hot, and everyone was very tired, and I nearly called over to Simon Warnock, our first assistant director, to ask him if he could please ask the gentleman to move aside and stop taking pictures. Then I realized it was the boss! He was just blending into the background and enjoying taking his photographs, and that's what was so terrific about it."

Jerry Bruckheimer also loves sports. On a routine basis he plays ice hockey with a collection of like-minded enthusiasts that he's pulled together, including both pro players and happy amateurs, and he organizes the annual Bad Boys Hockey Tournament in Las Vegas. He and his wife are also avid preservationists, working to maintain the architectural treasures of America. They have a particular interest in Linda's native Kentucky, where they maintain a magnificent spread of meticulously and lovingly restored old buildings, filled with antiques and Americana.

Jerry Bruckheimer is the first to confess that his winning streak would be inconceivable without collaboration. "If I'm successful, it's because I surround myself with the best creative people I can find, and then let them do their work," he insists. However, Bruckheimer has his finger on every switch of every project, and no detail is too small not to be scrutinized. From pre- to postproduction, as well as the shooting in between, the producer is deeply involved in all creative aspects of the film. "When we were editing *Remember the Titans*, after seeing the film for the first time, Jerry started giving the director incredibly precise notes off the top of his head," recalls Chad Oman. "He was changing the order of specific shots within scenes while also moving whole scenes around to restructure the story."

Says Mike Stenson, longtime president of Jerry Bruckheimer Films, "Jerry is like a great NBA coach. He puts an all-star team together, pushes for the best from everybody, and calls the plays. Jerry tends to be more hands-on than most producers, which is why, when you look at his body of work over a twenty-five-year period, there is a certain sensibility to it all."

"Jerry always has his own ideas," adds costume designer Penny Rose, whose collaboration with the producer has traversed all three Pirates of the Caribbean films as well as *King Arthur* and *Prince of Persia: The Sands of Time*. "He puts them out there, and if you want to stretch them a bit, or come up with a suggestion, he's always willing to listen. I'm extremely lucky to work with someone who is so visual and understanding of what you're doing. The visuals on Jerry's films are fantastic, because he understands every department from one end to the other."

The chorus of approval for Bruckheimer extends to the actors who have worked with him. "Jerry is sort of the great protector," explains Johnny Depp. "He wards off all and any evil spirits. And if anyone had anything really grave at stake in the beginning of Pirates, it was Jerry. Talk about rolling the dice. I mean, for an actor, you come in, do your bit, and if it works it works, and if it doesn't it doesn't, and it's on to the next one. But Jerry really took a risk."

The *Prince of Persia: The Sands of Time* cast seemed enthusiastic to be a part of a bona fide Jerry Bruckheimer blockbuster and quickly learned how the producer likes to make movies. "Working with Jerry has been a wonderful collaboration," says Jake Gyllenhaal. "He has given me a lot of say in my character, and gives everybody in the process the ability to do that. He has a very specific way of making movies that clearly has worked out pretty well for him, and it's an honor to be involved in one of his movies."

Alfred Molina has similar praise. "There's a difference in the air when you're working on a Jerry Bruckheimer movie," says the actor, who portrayed Sheikh Amar in *Prince of Persia: The Sands of Time* and then almost immediately segued into his role as the malevolent Maxim Horvath in *The Sorcerer's Apprentice*. "He's very much in charge, but he seems happy to delegate to people he trusts. He seems to say 'You've got the job, I trust you, so go and do your best.' And it's a good feeling, because the man whose name is on your checks actually has faith in what you're doing."

Toby Kebbell, who would also journey from *Prince of Persia: The Sands of Time* almost directly into *The Sorcerer's Apprentice*, says of the producer, "There's something absolutely special about his productions. Everything is geared towards making the film, there's nothing that feels superfluous. And that really gears you up to be dedicated to what you're doing. And the beauty of Mr. Bruckheimer is that he comes onto the sets, and he's like a kid, excited about the sets, costumes, and the story. It's inspiring."

Dame Helen Mirren, who starred in *National Treasure: Book of Secrets*, recently recalled in her autobiography *In the Frame*: "Jerry Bruckheimer, always dressed in black but with a nature that contradicted his sartorial choice, was gentle, supportive and courageous, proving the saying 'he who dares, wins' . . . Jerry never flinched or shouted or made anyone feel bad. He was shy and reserved, and utterly committed. I loved him."

But despite the box-office success, the honors, the accolades, and the almost endless procession of blockbusters on screens large and small, Bruckheimer is the last one to consider resting on his laurels. In fact, he openly admits that he's continually driven by fear of failure, an astonishing confession from a man who has spent nearly his entire professional life chalking up one success after another. "I don't look back and celebrate," he says. "I just always worry about the next one."

And what is the next one? It could either be the fourth installment of the Pirates of the Caribbean franchise, or a fresh and exciting new take on *The Lone Ranger*, both of which will reunite Bruckheimer with Johnny Depp (and yes, Kemo Sabe, Depp will return as Captain Jack Sparrow in the former and portray Tonto in the latter).

Perhaps the above-mentioned fear is the key to Jerry Bruckheimer's phenomenal creative output over the years. It gives him a relentless drive to reach a peak and then, rather than coast downhill from there, climb a higher hill. Appropriately, in that on-screen logo, when the lightning bolt hits the bare, lonely tree, it doesn't immolate it or split the tree in half. Instead, the tree immediately becomes covered with leaves. The lightning bolt is a force not of destruction, but of creation.

ABOVE: Dastan (Jake Gyllenhaal) and Tamina (Gemma Arterton) disguise their nobility with humble outfits while evading Nizam's troops in Alamut; OPPOSITE: Jerry Bruckheimer, an avid photographer, taking a picture (see page 30) of Gemma Arterton on the Alamut laundry set at Pinewood Studios.

OPPOSITE: A Moroccan extra on the Alamut exterior set in Tamesloht; ABOVE: Technicians position lights at a high altitude in the Atlas Mountains; RIGHT: Director of photography John Seale and gaffer Mo Flam check the sun's position in front of the temple on the Alamut exterior set.

OPPOSITE: Two Moroccan extras look as if they live on the meticulously detailed Alamut set in Tamesloht; ABOVE: Berber girl by the side of the road in the Atlas Mountains; RIGHT: A distinguished Moroccan background player in costume.

OPPOSITE ABOVE: *Moroccan background players take a break from the steaming midday sun on the Alamut exterior set; OPPOSITE BOTTOM: Gemma Arterton on the Alamut laundry set at Pinewood* Studios in England; *TOP: Sir Ben Kingsley and Richard Coyle on the Alamut Palace steps moments before the camera begins to turn; BOTTOM: A midday siesta for Moroccan background players.*

Looking Through The Kaleidoscope

In Mike Newell, Jerry Bruckheimer found a fellow dream-spinner determined to weave a world of magic, adventure, and romance. Newell proudly belongs to a classic breed of British filmmakers who, chameleon-like, seem to morph to accommodate whatever genre or subject captures their fancy. Newell has effortlessly shifted back and forth between the mainstream and independent film worlds for years, on both sides of the Atlantic, with such films to his credit as *Dance with a Stranger*, *Enchanted April*, *Pushing Tin*, and *Mona Lisa Smile*. Newell has also served as executive producer on such ambitious projects as Steven Soderbergh's *Traffic* and Stephen Frears's *High Fidelity*.

But if the subjects and backdrops have ranged far and wide, one common aspect in all of Newell's films has been his insistence on meticulously delineating the characters that inhabit the stories and giving free rein to the actors who portray them. Whether he's exploring the eminently and often hilariously human foibles of the multiple characters populating *Four Weddings and a Funeral*, the unforgettable relationship between Al Pacino's aging Mafia soldier and Johnny Depp's undercover policeman in *Donnie Brasco*, the tough professional and even tougher personal lives of New York City air traffic controllers in *Pushing Tin*, Julia Roberts's character's experiences as a progressive teacher trying to free her young female students' minds in *Mona Lisa Smile*, or even Harry Potter's considerable growing pains in *Goblet of Fire*, Mike Newell always focuses sharply on human nature, its heroism and folly—all of which were ripe for further exploration in *Prince of Persia: The Sands of Time*.

When presented by Jerry Bruckheimer with the invitation of directing *Prince of Persia*, Mike Newell saw a distinct opportunity to meld several of the genres in which he had previously worked with a new one for him: historical epic fantasy. "*Prince of Persia* is all of the categories that you would hope it to be," notes the filmmaker. "It's an exciting action film. It's a mystery. You're going to a place that you've never been before. It's a love story, and it's a comedy as well. But what I hope is that I take audiences to a new world, where the mysterious, the magical, and the mystical all co-exist.

"I don't know if this happens in American childhoods," continues Newell, "but every year at Christmas in England, you would find in your stocking a thing called a kaleidoscope. You would look through it, turn it, and there would be little glass beads that would form into fascinating shapes. I think of Prince of Persia as the most wonderful kaleidoscope of all."

"We all loved Mike's movies," says executive producer Mike Stenson. "He really understands actors, gets great performances, and has a great eye for casting. The question was whether he could pull off the spectacle, but in our opinion, he had directed one of the very best of the Harry Potter movies, so he had the experience of doing special effects and green screen work, and something very much in the world of pop culture. We felt like Mike could give us the performances and characters that were so important, but he had experience with the popcorn element as well."

"Jerry wanted a director who would really bring a sense of character and story," adds executive producer Chad Oman. "We felt that for the film to be successful, it had to be more than just a video game on the big screen. Mike Newell is extremely thoughtful and very respectful of everyone's opinion. At the same time, he runs the set like a commando unit. He doesn't like delays. And he doesn't like anyone who's not behaving professionally."

Like so many other highly successful pairings, producer Jerry Bruckheimer and director Mike Newell are a study in contrasts, men of different cultural backgrounds who found common ground in a shared goal: to bring *Prince of Persia: The Sands of Time* to the screen. Newell is English to his very roots, addressing friends and colleagues alike with such affectionate "Britishisms" as "old chap," "love," "sweetheart," and "darling," and he is quite familiar with the attire of a gentleman (and completely comfortable wearing it on set). With his booming, stentorian voice, carefully detailed direction, and daunting erudition

and intellect, he comes across like a Cambridge don who has decided to segue from the lecture hall into the director's chair.

Well into the five-month shoot, Sir Ben Kingsley would reflect upon working with Mike Newell: "Because it's technically so complex, the method of making the film involves us doing tiny portions of a scene in isolation. In some cases, we continue shooting a scene that we started in Morocco months later at Pinewood Studios. And we have to have the same tone, same temperature, same emotional heartbeat that we had a long time before. And we as human beings have changed, but Mike Newell is a wonderful conductor in that he makes the orchestra play exactly the same notes that they played months before. He can remember exactly where we left off, and he can translate it into language that the actor thrives on. It's really helpful and very embracing."

Sir Ben's fellow cast members chime in with their own chorus of approval for their director. "Mike is just wonderful, so smart and robust," says Jake Gyllenhaal. "Mike is all about performance and story, and that's his strength. Also, his sense of comedy is really wonderful, very dry and British. When he tells me something, particularly in a comedic moment, it's always based in a real place."

"I adore Mike," enthuses Gemma Arterton. "He's got such tremendous energy, is an actor's director, and is also a great storyteller. He has real respect for actors, so he gives you time to do what you need. He's got great humor, and a real English eccentricity . . . which, being English, I love. We have good fun on set."

Alfred Molina, who had worked with Newell on *Enchanted April* some sixteen years before their reunion on *Prince of Persia: The Sands of Time*, has come to know his director well.

"I'll tell you what Mike brings, apart from an extraordinary amount of experience, knowledge, and taste, and a real sense of someone who knows how to take charge and run the room. I've always thought that filming is basically a benevolent dictatorship. In fact, there's nothing democratic about making films. There has to be someone who everyone else can look to and say, 'Well, now what?' And that person has to be strong enough and prepared enough to say exactly what they need. You look for someone who can run the team, and Mike does that very easily. He carries that responsibility very lightly, because he loves what he does. He comes impeccably prepared, and he's generous with his time and efforts. Mike's experience with big films really tells in that situation, but, at the same time, he's also a director who started on small films. He knows the importance of the scene involving two people talking in a room, and understands that there's a dynamic to that as well as seeing thousands of soldiers charging across the landscape on horseback."

Toby Kebbell uses a cultural metaphor in describing Mike Newell. "For me, as an Englishman, he has a manner of what I imagine to be a headmaster. Mike has genuine power, but he's rarely forceful. On such massive sets, to give you a note, he could easily sit in a chair and shout through a megaphone, but he comes over, talks to you, congratulates you on what he likes and asks you for more of what he didn't quite get from you. Mike's a very eclectic person, with sources of information from everywhere. He's one of the brightest men I've ever met, and a great storyteller, which is what I really feel a director should be."

OPPOSITE: Mike Newell and Jake Gyllenhaal share a laugh in "video village" on location in Morocco; ABOVE: Mike Newell in command of his troops on another hot Moroccan day.

PART TWO

shining stars

Dastan

What qualities make a hero? The role of Dastan required an actor who could be multi-layered: at once dashing in the classic-movie mode and wily, with a sense of raffish fun befitting a "trickster," but also burdened with the underlying gravitas of poverty and driven by aspirations to become a better man. The only logical choice was a young artist of the first rank, and Jake Gyllenhaal had already demonstrated his serious acting chops in such films as Ang Lee's *Brokeback Mountain* and David Fincher's *Zodiac*.

"Jake Gyllenhaal is an actor I've been watching and wanting to work with for a very long time," says Jerry Bruckheimer, "ever since I saw him years ago in one of his first television films. He's a wonderful actor, exceedingly handsome, and a great gentleman. Jake is also incredibly dedicated. He did an amazing job training himself for *Prince of Persia*, putting on an enormous amount of muscle; fight-training; sword fighting; parkour training; horse riding. And he continued to work out and train every single day of the more than one-hundred-day shoot."

"I've known Jake a very long time," says Mike Newell, "since he was a little boy. He was always very curious, interested in everything. And then, to my astonishment, both he and his sister Maggie turned into actors, and they're both very good at it. I worked with Maggie in *Mona Lisa Smile*."

"I considered lots of actors for Dastan," Newell continues, "but Jake has a man-of-the-people quality. He's curious, open, gentle, very tough, and has great comic abilities, and in *Prince of Persia*, he uses all of that. I saw pretty much everything he had made, and thought him a marvelous actor, with terrific charisma. But what I didn't know about Jake was that he would be an absolutely God-given action hero. He can fight, hold a sword, run, clamber, jump, and ride a horse as if he were glued to the back of it. And that I didn't expect. I expected the acting and the good looks, but didn't know that he could hold a sword and look like he means it—and that's not a small thing."

Gyllenhaal also received a ringing endorsement from the man who created the prince: Jordan Mechner. "Any time you have a character who an audience has connected to through another medium, whether it's a novel or a video game, people are going to have strong feelings about it. But I think that if you have a good actor and a good movie, then after the first minute it's no longer an issue. I think Jake is a fantastic choice for the role. Once you see him in costume and in action, you have no doubt that he can be the prince in sixth-century Persia."

From a historical perspective, Mechner points out that "there were Persians who were as fair-skinned as Jake, there were Persians who were Asian, there were Persians who were black. You can't cast one person who represents all of an empire as ethnically diverse as Persia was. The movie is based on the

Sands of Time game, but if you look at all of the games from the Apple II version to the present time, the prince looks a little bit different. The artists put their own stamp on each version—and, in fact, in some of them he's an entirely different character—yet they all somehow embody the same archetype and spirit. But for the movie, you need one flesh-and-blood human being. Jake definitely looks like the prince, but more important than how an actor looks is who they are, and the personality they project. Jake is strong, heroic, humorous, sensitive, and vulnerable, and you have no doubt he's going to do the right thing."

When offered the role by Bruckheimer and Newell, Jake Gyllenhaal was overwhelmed by the sheer scope of the project. "When I read the script, at first I thought, Wow, I've never been involved in something that huge, and wondered how it could be pulled off. *Prince of Persia: The Sands of Time* was just so different from anything that I had been involved in. I thought that creating an iconic character like Dastan could be both fun and a huge challenge. I've always loved movies in which the hero has the capability to do almost anything but still be a human being, and not a superman."

Gyllenhaal was intrigued by the character and his myriad aspects. "Dastan has evolved as we've been making the movie," he observed at Pinewood Studios near the end of the marathon shoot, "and what I love about him most is his sense of humor. Dastan always has a trick up his sleeve, always has a plan. He's a kid from the streets, and it's his heart and his goodness that bring him into the court of King Sharaman. And from that point on, Dastan is constantly being thrust into circumstances that seem impossible to get out of, and yet he always does. And every time that happens, he discovers that somebody else is not what they seem, and Dastan has to get all the way back to the person he was as a little boy to find the prince that he is. It's a very simple story, but with so many complex turns.

"The development of the character was massively physical at first," Gyllenhaal continues, "just getting in shape, learning parkour, how to sword-fight, learning the mentality of a warrior. I knew that if I got through that I'd be halfway there. And when it was decided that Dastan would speak in a standard British accent to be consistent with the rest of the performers, I worked hard at that as well with a dialect coach named Barbara Berkery."

Having acted professionally since his teens, Jake Gyllenhaal has been working hard at his craft for most of his twenty-eight years (his age at the time of filming.) And it seems that no two roles he's played have been alike. "Jake really made his bones as a lead actor who specialized in character and immersing himself in his roles," notes executive producer Mike Stenson. Following his early career performances in such films as Joe Johnston's *October Sky*, Gyllenhaal expanded his profile in such films as Richard Kelly's cult favorite *Donnie Darko*, Nicole Holofcener's *Lovely & Amazing*, and Miguel Arteta's *The Good Girl*—all exemplars of independent American cinema. He further stretched his acting muscles with diverse performances in *Moonlight Mile*, *The Day After Tomorrow*, and *Proof*.

It was, however, Gyllenhaal's heartbreakingly poignant performance in Ang Lee's *Brokeback Mountain*, opposite the late Heath Ledger, that represented a quantum leap for the actor. For his role as conflicted cowboy Jack Twist, Gyllenhaal won the 2006 Best Supporting Actor awards from both the British Academy of Film and Television Arts (BAFTA) and the National Board of Review. His portrayal also earned nominations for an Academy Award and a Screen Actors Guild Award. He followed up with ambitious and well received performances in Sam Mendes's *Jarhead*, David Fincher's critically acclaimed *Zodiac*, and Gavin Hood's *Rendition*.

For Jake Gyllenhaal, the challenges and daily rigors of making *Prince of Persia: The Sands of Time* were completely worthwhile. "Every time I walk onto one of the sets in this movie, I just think of all the children that I know and love, and how much fun they're going to have watching this movie," he says. "The fact is, I made it for them. And if I'm frustrated about something, I take a look at the sets of Alamut, or the Sandglass of the Gods, and I just think about how much fun the kids are going to have watching Dastan fight off the Hassansins and doing his jumps and leaps. It brings me a lot of joy to think about that, because I remember how huge of an influence movie heroes had on my life when I was young. Kids today are brought up in a very different world. We're experiencing a lot of hard stuff. So it's really nice to have a movie that's going to be a real escape and a metaphor for them that represents good. It's a nice feeling to be a part of something like that."

I think Jake is a fantastic choice for the role. Once you see him in costume and in action, you have no doubt that he can be the prince in sixth-century Persia.

— *Jordan Mechner*

CREATING THE DAGGER OF TIME

Of all the thousands of items under the domain of property master David Balfour, none was more important than the single most iconic object in the film: the Dagger of Time. Nothing less than a bladed time machine, the Dagger contains sands that hurtle its possessor on a journey to the past. It is also the only device that can cut through the crystal of the Sandglass of the Gods. These factors make the Dagger a hotly contested item.

As was the case with nearly everything in the movie, creating the final version of the Dagger of Time was a process of research, development, and experimentation. "Initially, we'd looked at an old-style Indian dagger as a model," notes Balfour, a laconic Scotsman with nearly fifty credits to his name, an eternally dry sense of humor, and a mighty reputation in his field. "But Jerry Bruckheimer wanted the Dagger to more closely resemble the one in the video game. The problem was that the hilt of the Dagger from the game, when turned into something three-dimensional, didn't seem to be able to perform the functions that it had to do in the film. We had to do a bit of work to redesign the hilt, with its glass handle, metal filigree, and jewel button on top that releases the sand from the blade."

"I think the end result was successful," continues Balfour. "The handle is still elegant, as it was in the game, and we enhanced the blade with a lot of engraving." In fact, the Alamutian inscription on the blade of the Dagger translates as "Our lives are forever in the hands of the Gods," an appropriate sentiment considering its spiritual power. Balfour created some twenty different versions of the Dagger of Time, all identical but serving different functions. "The 'hero' version actually has a metal blade," explains Balfour. "It's fabricated from brass and is gold-plated. The weight is there, and it's picture quality." There was a considerable amount of maintenance that had to be constantly performed on the hero version of the Dagger, because of the film's many action sequences. "It's thrown around, kicked out of Dastan's hands, knocked into the dirt," says Balfour. "There's a lot that goes on with the Dagger, so it's had its fair share of repairs. But we also had exact duplicates made in both hard and soft rubber for stunts, and one that actually lights up."

Tamina's amulet, which carries the Sands of Time, "is close to the design of the hilt of the dagger," says Balfour, "with the same swirling bands of metal around it."

As for the magical Sands of Time, Balfour, after much research, decided upon tiny glass beads that reflect light in a shimmering, supernatural way. "We got two different grades of beads," explains chargehand standby propsman Bradley Torbett, "one for when the sand is passing through the Dagger, and another that's inside the glass hilt. What we've done is to give Tom Wood and his visual-effects department a base to start with, for what they'll later enhance."

In what mystical realm were these marvelous glass beads manufactured? Columbia, Tennessee!

LEFT and RIGHT: Concept illustrations of Tamina's amulet, which contains the Sands of Time, and the Dagger of Time. Much refinement took place before their designs were finalized.

GEMMA ARTERTON
Tamina

If it can be said that 2008 was the Year of Gemma Arterton, it can also be suggested that there are undoubtedly many more of those years still to come. Demonstrating her head-spinning versatility, the transcendently lovely young Briton portrayed not only the title role in the BBC four-part adaptation of Thomas Hardy's *Tess of the D'Urbervilles*, but also the fetching Agent Shields opposite Daniel Craig's 007 in *Quantum of Solace*. She also starred, along with Philip Seymour Hoffman, Bill Nighy, and Kenneth Branagh, in Richard Curtis's raucous comedy *Pirate Radio* (aka *The Boat That Rocked*). Previously, after graduating from the Royal Academy of Dramatic Arts (RADA) in the summer of 2007, Arterton made her feature-film debut as a hellion schoolgirl in *St. Trinian's*, appeared as Rosaline in *Love's Labour's Lost* at Shakespeare's Globe Theatre, and was seen on television in the BBC's *Capturing Mary* and in ITV's *Lost in Austen*.

2008 was also the year in which, after a worldwide search, Gemma Arterton was summoned by Jerry Bruckheimer and Mike Newell to star as Tamina in *Prince of Persia: The Sands of Time*. "Gemma is a wonderful young actress who we found in London, a recent graduate of the Royal Academy of Dramatic Arts," says Jerry Bruckheimer. "She had a small part in *Quantum of Solace*, and we cast her before that picture hit the big screen, so we feel very fortunate that we got in on the ground floor, because she's been turning a lot of heads ever since the Bond film was released. Gemma is going to be a really big star."

"Our casting director, Susie Figgis, suggested that I meet Gemma," recalls Mike Newell, "and I absolutely loved her. She's beautiful, of course, but she has a tremendous kind of outgoingness, because she's a working-class girl, not a posh girl at all. That means a lot in this country. And Gemma comes from down the river, which, again, in this country, means a lot. When she first came to see me, Gemma spoke with a strong working-class accent. She was absolutely lovely and very interesting for the part. I asked, 'Can you do posh talking?' and she said: 'Oh, yes, I was at the Royal Academy of Dramatic Arts.'

"And what I loved about her," continues Newell, "was that— and long may she retain the quality—she had none of those layers of artifice, defense, and arrogance that very quickly build up in a young actor who quickly becomes successful."

"Susie Figgis looked all over the world for our Tamina," says Chad Oman. "Gemma was, hands down, the best choice. But we screen-tested her a couple of times just to make sure, and she was great every time. What she brought to the table was a real gregariousness. Gemma's very confident and funny in real life, and brought all of that to Tamina."

"The first time we all saw Gemma," adds Mike Stenson, "we thought that she was gorgeous, but at the same time she had a real strength and edge, which the part requires. The princess has

Tamina is more than a typical action figure. She's spiritual, very wise, thoughtful, and sensitive as well. But she also gives the guys a run for their money, and really kicks some butt.

— *Gemma Arterton*

to stand up to all of the guys in the movie and give as good as she gets. Gemma absolutely was that girl." And the fact that Arterton was, at the time, nearly a complete unknown didn't sway either the Bruckheimer or Newell camp. "There was no compelling reason for us to cast Keira Knightley in *Pirates of the Caribbean*," recalls Stenson. "She had only done *Bend It Like Beckham* at that point, but we all felt that as an actor, she could bring a strength to the role of Elizabeth Swann. And the rest is history."

In her role as Tamina, a princess and a priestess, protector and defender of the Dagger of Time, Gemma Arterton had to project qualities both ethereal and earthy. She accomplished this task with ease, barely seeming to break a sweat in the process (even in the withering heat of Morocco in mid-summer). As for Arterton, she just loved the idea of being in a big, booming, Jerry Bruckheimer epic.

"The scale of it, creating a new world on-screen, something that's never been done before, and the action, were really exciting to me," Arterton recalled towards the end of the shoot. "I've always wanted to do an action movie, and kind of fancied myself as a bit of a stunt girl. When I first heard about the film, though, I never thought I'd get it. I hadn't yet done *Quantum of Solace*, so being cast in an even bigger film was a far-fetched idea."

Not all that far-fetched, as things turned out. And Arterton was eager to tackle the ambitious role, which is central to the whole grand enterprise. "Tamina is a high priestess and princess of Alamut, as well as the protector of the Dagger of Time, so she has to carry a lot of responsibility," Arterton explains of her character. "She believes that her destiny is to protect the Dagger no matter what, but that changes when she meets and eventually falls in love with Dastan. When you fall for someone, everything goes out the window, so there's a really interesting journey that she and Dastan make together. When they interact, they both eventually change each other. Tamina learns to relax a bit, and Dastan learns to open his mind.

"She's a great character for me to play," Arterton continues, "because Tamina is more than a typical action figure. She's spiritual, very wise, thoughtful, and sensitive as well. The most beautiful thing about Tamina is that she's a character with faith, and really believes in what she's trying to do. But she also gives the guys a run for their money, and really kicks some butt.

"Tamina is also very witty," Arterton adds, "and I like to compare the relationship between Dastan and Tamina to that of Beatrice and Benedick in Shakespeare's *Much Ado About Nothing*. Tamina is intelligent, funny, and has a sharp tongue, so she's a great role model for young women."

The initially hostile and often combative relationship between Dastan and Tamina gave Jake Gyllenhaal and Gemma Arterton ample opportunity to sharpen their verbal claws in scenes together. "Jake is a naturally humorous person, so we had lots of banter anyway, which kind of fed into what we were doing in front of the camera," observes Arterton. "We'd muck about on set, and Jake is easy to bounce off of in that respect, because he's a funny guy. But at the same time, because he's a good actor, we could get through to all of the undertones of Dastan and Tamina's relationship, so it was brilliant. I was really lucky to act opposite Jake."

Jake Gyllenhaal and the other stars of the film certainly felt the same way about Arterton. "Gemma has been given massive opportunities so early in her career," says Gyllenhaal, "and has really dealt with them very well. I think that her ability to keep her mind around the huge scope of the film, and also to create a character within that, is amazing. She really pulled it off, in all the best ways."

"Gemma is a great leading lady," enthuses Sir Ben Kingsley. "She's a wonderful presence on set, and a very accomplished actor."

"*Prince of Persia: The Sands of Time* is mystical, and magical, and like nothing else that you've seen for a long time, I think," says Arterton. "It's got comedy, adventure, romance, a serious story line, really deep characters. So I think it's just going to appeal to everybody."

BEN KINGSLEY
Nizam

How ironic that the actor portraying the darkest character in *Prince of Persia: The Sands of Time*—Dastan's morally conflicted uncle, Nizam, the brother of Dastan's adoptive father, King Sharaman—should have been attracted to the role for the most illuminating of reasons. But then again, Sir Ben Kingsley, one of Britain's (and the world's) most distinguished and accomplished actors, has never followed a prescribed path.

"What appealed to me about the story is the notion that everybody has great potential," states Sir Ben. "And this is where I thought it would be a very affirming film, particularly for young people—to realize that whilst you might be a child of the streets,

it doesn't mean that your potential is any less than that of a child from the palace. Our film is an examination of the potential of a child coming into adulthood, and the choices that that child has.

"Therefore, the forces have to be set against the child in order for the story to be entertaining, and you see him overcome these hurdles and become the man he was destined to be, and the different aspects of that struggle are very appealing. As Nizam, I am a dark and challenging aspect. In other words, without my character in the story, Dastan would never grow up. For me, it isn't like playing the baddie—it's playing a very essential force that's completely locked into the story, the narrative, the myth of the film."

Sir Ben Kingsley's great erudition, insight, and overwhelming skill as an actor made him a clear and perfect choice to portray Nizam, the man who would be king—if he hadn't saved his brother, Sharaman, heir to the throne, from a lion attack when they were boys. "You always try to populate your film with fantastic actors," says Jerry Bruckheimer. "And when you get somebody like Sir Ben Kingsley, you're very fortunate to be able to entice him to do the project. He was, in every way, the perfect choice to play Nizam."

"Nizam is the man who Dastan believes is his friend, his mentor—somebody who is utterly dependable, affectionate, and will always help him," explains Mike Newell. "Ben is a big actor, and he can see a good part when you show it to him. I thought there were two movies to be made: the main movie, and then the secret movie—which is the Nizam movie. You have to be very careful to be restrained about the way you tell that second movie, but of course, Ben loved the idea that one of them was his and his alone."

"Sir Ben Kingsley's work speaks for itself," offers Jake Gyllenhaal, "which of course is why he's here. He's just an extraordinary actor in all respects and all rights, and has earned all the accolades that any actor could or would ever hope to, and we're just lucky to have him in our film. That's how I feel every day I'm working with him. He's incredibly sensitive, and I liked seeing that in someone who's so experienced. He hasn't been hardened to a life of acting in movies and onstage. He's ever learning and ever curious to what's happening, and I really respect that he could be so open to a twenty-eight-year-old actor who's still at the beginning of his career, and just be kind and giving."

"My character appealed to me," Sir Ben says, "because of two very clear ideas that the actor can focus on, which are envy and regret: Envy that, when he is in public, all eyes are on his brother; and regret that, when he had an opportunity to allow his brother to die, he didn't take it. He saved his brother's life. Envy and regret are the opposite of potential and hope, so it's a beautiful balance between Jake's character and mine, and at the center, if you like, is the lovely princess, played by Gemma, who holds everything in balance. She's like the good angel in the middle, holding destiny in her hand, and quite willing to sacrifice herself for those goals to be fulfilled. So I think that our wonderful director, Mike Newell, has examined a beautifully crafted, plot-driven script, and then infused it with individual character struggles."

Sir Ben Kingsley, who earned his knighthood as a result of nearly three decades of brilliant work on screen and stage, is a man who projects, all at the same time, deep intelligence, warmth, elegance, and austerity. A native of Yorkshire, England, he joined the Royal Shakespeare Company in 1967 and excelled

at playing numerous characters created by the Bard, including the title roles in both *Othello* and *Hamlet*. Although he made his feature-film debut in 1972, it was Sir Ben's serendipitous casting by Richard Attenborough as the Mahatma in 1982's Best Picture Oscar-winner, *Gandhi*, that propelled him to international fame. For his performance, Sir Ben earned an Academy Award, two Golden Globes, and two British Academy of Film and Television Arts (BAFTA) Awards; he then went on to garner three additional Oscar nominations for his roles as the gangster Meyer Lansky in *Bugsy* (1991), the terrifying mobster Don Logan in *Sexy Beast* (2000), and Colonel Behrani, a proud Iranian living in U.S. exile, in *House of Sand and Fog* (2003).

Ben Kingsley's catalog of screen portrayals is extraordinarily diverse. Whether portraying the vice president of the United States in *Dave*, the scheming Fagin in Roman Polanski's version of *Oliver Twist*, the drug-addled shrink in *The Wackness*, the love-besotted professor in *Elegy*, or Itzhak Stern, the moral conscience in Steven Spielberg's seven-time Oscar-winner *Schindler's List*, the actor has meticulously worked his way into the very soul of his characters. He was knighted by Queen Elizabeth II in the New Year's Eve Honors List in 2001. Sir Ben takes

this royal acknowledgment quite seriously, and uses it to the best possible purpose in his charitable endeavors.

As with every film he has made, Sir Ben looked for and discovered the heart of *Prince of Persia: The Sands of Time*. "The film is, by definition, an epic," he says. "And it will have enormous cavalry charges, sieges against huge fortresses, and the most splendid palaces you've ever seen on the screen. It will also have chambers beneath the palaces that go towards the actual Sandglass of the Gods itself, so it explores both what's above and beneath the surface.

"And that's not only epic, but also a beautiful metaphor for what goes on both on the surface of ourselves as human beings, and what's really going on inside, which can sometimes be two very different things. I think the film says many things. . . . It certainly suggests that everything happens for a reason. So, every time you're looking at a gaggle of street kids, whether in the slums of Rio de Janeiro, South Africa, or India, remember that at least one of them could have the soul of a prince inside of them. Don't throw young children away. They are so precious. In any world, developed or not, children are a resource. Any of these kids could be a prince."

Sheikh Amar

"Nothing is beneath him," says Jerry Bruckheimer, not of Alfred Molina—a consummate professional and gentleman known to friends and colleagues as Fred—but of the character he so richly portrays in *Prince of Persia: The Sands of Time*. That character is a scurrilous, unscrupulous, but undeniably charismatic *capo di tutti capi* among desert thieves who goes by the name of Sheikh Amar. "Whatever Alfred Molina plays is totally believable, and whatever he touches with his talent turns to absolute screen gold," Bruckheimer notes. "He can be scary and hilarious nearly at the same time, which is exactly what the role of Sheikh Amar called for."

"Sheikh Amar runs a racing empire, but he runs ostriches rather than horses," says director Mike Newell. "In his own head, he's built this colossal kind of Las Vegas in the middle of the Arabian desert. It isn't. It's a skuzzy little outfit, but nonetheless, for him, it's huge. I worked with Alfred Molina before, on a film called *Enchanted April*, had a wonderful time, and thought this would be a great opportunity to reunite on a completely different kind of film in which he plays a completely different kind of character."

"He's a sort of roguish opportunist," says Molina of his character. "He really doesn't care whether he breaks the law. He's quite dangerous at times. Sheikh Amar describes himself as an entrepreneur. His methods are unusual, unconventional, and he's basically a thief. But although he starts off as sort of a bad guy, Sheikh Amar becomes a reluctant ally of Dastan, and in the end, they join up and have the same quest, although for very different reasons."

Although the sheikh may be a less-than-savory individual, Molina's characterization is leavened by considerable dollops of humor, provided both by the script and by the actor's endless inventiveness. "Seso, who is played by Steve Toussaint, is the sheikh's right-hand man," Molina explains. "They have a background together, the result of which is that Seso feels beholden to the sheikh and is, metaphorically speaking, willing to take a bullet for him. There's a real sense, though, that Seso doesn't just work for the sheikh, but is really a friend." Life would imitate art, as Molina and Toussaint indeed became good friends over the course of filming. "Sheikh Amar is amoral, but Fred is not," states Toussaint. "He's a very funny and warm man, very easy and fun to work with. There's genuine affection between Amar and Seso, and there certainly is between Fred and I. It's been a dream working with him."

Sheikh Amar's relationship with Dastan throughout the

story takes unexpected and precipitous turns. "I think it veers from the sheikh first seeing Dastan as an enemy, then some kind of protégé, then a kind of ally, and finally, in a way, Dastan becomes the boss," Molina explains. "It keeps evolving, which is really what makes it good storytelling."

Although Sheikh Amar lives in a dangerous world, he's really not much of a warrior. Not only is he a bit of a chicken, but during the battle with the Hassansins in the Hidden Valley, he literally hides behind a chicken coop. "This is an interesting element to the sheikh, and it's one of the reasons why I quite enjoyed the idea of playing this part," says Molina. "He comes across as a kind of dangerous, scary character, and there are a lot of scenes in which we see him sitting on a horse, brandishing a sword, and threatening people. But then, when push comes to shove, he's actually a bit of a physical coward. He's wily, cunning, calculating, street-smart, an opportunist, so the sheikh's decision not to get involved in too much physical violence is calculated. He's surrounded by people who can do that for him."

Sheikh Amar saves most of his true affection for his beloved, racing ostriches (see sidebar), but Alfred Molina had a great deal of affection for the difficult locations in which much of the film was shot. "Filming in Morocco was pretty intense, and very interesting because of the range of conditions. We worked up in the mountains, had the heat of the desert, starting off in the spring and working into the height of summer when it was very, very hot. But it was such an extraordinarily beautiful place—quite stunning and very rewarding visually.

"I'm reluctant to say it was 'tough,'" Molina continues. "Working in a mine or a steel plant is tough. Shooting in Morocco was very invigorating and exhilarating. I actually loved it. We also had a fantastic group of actors to work with, a wonderful range of age, experience, and background. You create a family when you work together on distant locations that are testing and challenging. You live together and rely on each other . . . not just in terms of the work, but also, when you're off duty, you keep each other company. It's so great when the chemistry works, and this is a very generous group of people."

No small part of that chemistry was due to Molina's talents. The British-born son of a Spanish father and Italian mother, Alfred Molina is a wonderfully gifted actor whose mind-boggling versatility has seen him portraying a remarkable gallery of characters on-screen since his debut as Indiana Jones's doomed guide in the opening sequence of *Raiders of the Lost Ark*. Perhaps most notable among his roles was his portrayal of Dr. Otto Octavius (aka Doc Ock), opposite Tobey Maguire in Sam Raimi's *Spider-Man 2*. Molina never lost sight of the man behind the monster in that film, creating a villain all the more poignant and powerful for his errant humanity.

Molina's other big-screen roles have included the larger-than-life Mexican artist Diego Rivera in Julie Taymor's *Frida*

(soon after *Persia* filming wrapped, he was summoned by the director to portray Stephano in her version of Shakespeare's *The Tempest*); playwright Joe Orton's lover (and murderer) Kenneth Halliwell in *Prick Up Your Ears*; the abusive Moody in *Not Without My Daughter*; Rahad Jackson in *Boogie Nights*; Bishop Manuel Aringarosa in *The Da Vinci Code*; and the morally compromised Dick Suskind in *The Hoax*. Onstage, Molina has excelled in numerous West End and other British productions, and received two Tony Award nominations for his Broadway roles in both Yasmina Reza's *Art* (which brought him a Drama Desk Award) and David Leveaux's 2004 production of the classic musical *Fiddler on the Roof* in which he played Tevye.

On the set of *Prince of Persia: The Sands of Time*, Molina was much beloved by all for his seemingly endless good nature and high spirits—even in the face of the intense heat, dust storms, and inevitable tummy troubles that assailed the company. "There's not a single person on this movie who can find a bad thing to say about Fred Molina," says Jake Gyllenhaal. "He's just great, an actor's actor who adds light and life to the movie. Fred raised the bar, and he's just a lovely man."

"Fred is so incredible, quick—a comic genius," adds Gemma Arterton. "He's a naturally funny and warm person who was always making us laugh." Molina certainly made quite an impression on producer Jerry Bruckheimer, who promptly cast Molina in his very next production for Walt Disney Pictures. Molina would go on to play the vengeful Maxim Horvath opposite Nicolas Cage in the romantic comedy adventure *The Sorcerer's Apprentice*.

While some consider the theme of *Prince of Persia: The Sands of Time* to be destiny, Molina believes that "it's more to do with affirming the need to survive with some kind of honor and decency. Dastan's background is humble, and through an amazing stroke of good fortune, he comes to enjoy a wonderful life. He loves the man who was his adoptive father and his life with his stepbrothers. And then all of that is besmirched, and Dastan is suddenly perceived as a villain.

"After that, he's after clearing his name," Molina continues. "He's not after money, he's not after self-improvement, he's not after the boss's job. He's after some kind of decency, and to repair the damage and bring things back to the way they were. This manages to be a very domestic and, at the same time, an incredibly epic theme, which strikes me as more Shakespearean than anything else.

"I think it's rather presumptuous of us to imagine that audiences are going to come out of watching *Prince of Persia* and be better people for it," Molina concludes. "If an audience walks out thinking that their ten bucks have been really well spent, then we've done our job. If they come out entertained and uplifted in some way . . . if it makes them curious about wanting to find out more about history . . . that's even better!"

BIG BIRD, OR HOW I LEARNED TO STOP WORRYING AND LOVE THE OSTRICH

There's no question about it. Ostriches seem to have a really terrible reputation for being ornery, smelly, scary, and downright dangerous, which might explain why the otherwise visually interesting critters, who so closely resemble (and behave like) their prehistoric ancestors, have rarely been featured on-screen.

But Jerry Bruckheimer and Mike Newell change all that with *Prince of Persia: The Sands of Time*, which contains an elaborate and highly original scene involving the big, clumsy, but oddly majestic birds. The sequence was filmed amid the otherworldly jagged stones of Bouaissoun, a rough but wondrous natural landscape forty-five kilometers northwest of Marrakesh. This is where Sheikh Amar (portrayed by Alfred Molina) has built his gloriously ramshackle ostrich-racing amphitheater, hosting spectacles attended by his motley crew of desert brigands and every other dubious soul for miles around. On the run from the entire Persian army, Dastan and Tamina perhaps foolishly enter the Valley of the Slaves, which is under the control of the desert rats, and they become the sheikh's less-than-enthusiastic "guests" at the ostrich race.

"I never thought that ostriches would ever end up in one of my films," declares Jerry Bruckheimer, "but it's really a hysterically funny sequence."

Two ostrich experts were brought in to supervise: Bill Rivers, who hails from San Antonio, Texas, and Jennifer Henderson, from Orlando, Florida. Stunt coordinator George Aguilar and his team—with Rivers's assistance—enlisted eight professional Moroccan jockeys to ride the ostriches. But before filming could begin, they would have to train for two solid weeks. "None of the jockeys ever rode an ostrich before," says Rivers in the steamy heat of the Bouaissoun location, incongruously wearing an all-American cowboy hat and imposing rodeo-style belt buckle. "It's a lot different than riding a horse, because ostriches have only two legs, and they're not as stable. It takes a lot of practice. If you sit too far forward, you're going to take a tumble, and sometimes an ostrich will run right into the fences. You also have to dismount properly so you don't get run over, kicked, or stepped on."

Sounds like fun, right? Just ask Youssef El Mouatani, Mohamed Amine Elkhoulimi, Abdeslam Assif, Salah Azaddou, El Housseine Barkhous, Anouar Amaach, Youssef Afroukh, and Abdelhak Ait Mazouz. They're the ostrich riders, all from Marrakesh.

"Well, most of the jockeys have done really well," says Rivers. "Of course, they're used to riding racehorses, which can be tricky because they're so fired up all the time. But riding the ostriches takes a little more skill and balance, because they're a little more wobbly up on top."

Perhaps ostrich racing is a Disney tradition, because the only other such cinematic sequence that anyone could recall was in the Studio's classic 1960 version of *Swiss Family Robinson* (the great Mexican comic actor Cantinflas also briefly rode an ostrich for transportation in the 1956 version of *Around the World in 80 Days*). And confirming that these things run in the family, Bill Rivers's father-in-law was the ostrich wrangler on *Swiss Family Robinson*. But those scenes were small peanuts compared to the races in *Prince of Persia: The Sands of Time*. And what's more, the races would be absolutely unscripted in terms of who made it to the finish line.

"What you see in the movie is a real ostrich race, which is the fun of it," notes Jennifer Henderson. "We don't know who's going to win, and what riders are going to manage to stay on."

The ostriches used in *Prince of Persia: The Sands of Time* hailed from a farm in Rabat, the capital city of Morocco. Members of the Blue Neck breed, the twenty birds lived on the set while the racetrack and adjacent pens were being built, allowing them to get acclimated to their surroundings. "We've homed them in one pen at the top of the racetrack, and that's where they live," notes Henderson. "Then they finish at a second pen at the bottom of the track. We make sure that they're comfortable, safe, and cool."

Justifiably, there was a stern warning on the top of each day's call sheet whenever the birds were working: STRICTLY ALL CAST/CREW DO NOT TOUCH THE OSTRICHES ON SET TODAY. THESE ANIMALS CAN BE DANGEROUS.

"They have a big claw on their feet," advises Henderson, "and if they kick, they can cut you very badly."

If only for their imposing size and strength, ostriches seem rather noble, don't they? "Oh, they're dumber than a rock," responds Bill Rivers with a grin and a Texas drawl. "Their eyeball is bigger than their brain."

Not all of the actors involved in the sequence were eager to become well acquainted with the ostriches. "Uh, I didn't get very close to them," admits Steve Toussaint, who plays the warrior Seso. "If you were unfortunate enough to see one of them respond to nature's call, that's something that would stay with you for the rest of your life. Very disturbing."

But at least one notable personage on the *Prince of Persia* set—perhaps immersing himself in his character slightly more than was absolutely required—learned to love the long-legged beasties. "I don't think we've seen a member of the human species being quite so emotionally involved with an ostrich," says Alfred Molina with a chuckle. "I think we're breaking new ground here."

In the film, Dastan and Tamina's escape from the sheikh's clutches results in chaos on the racetrack, with Amar's ostriches escaping in all directions. Later, when the sheikh once again encounters Dastan and Tamina at a desert oasis, only one ostrich is still with him. "That's my very, very special one, Anita, who is sort of a star of Sheikh Amar's ostrich empire," reveals Molina. "I show off Anita to Dastan, and talk to him lovingly about this particular ostrich. Because these animals are very unpredictable and rather sort of quixotic in their movements and decisions, I had noticed, watching Jennifer Henderson, that she would constantly stroke their necks to keep them calm. So I thought, Well I'll try that, maybe it will help the scene.

"I was praying that Anita would be still, so I stroked her neck—which was actually very soft and sinewy— did the dialogue, and it went beautifully for two or three takes. And then, on one take—and I don't know what possessed me—but in the middle of the dialogue praising Anita, I just leaned forward and kissed her on the neck, thinking that I would either get my eye poked out or get away with it. And it went great! But at the end of the day, Jennifer told me that Anita, who I thought was a female, was actually Alan, a male. So I think that we did the first sort of gay, interspecies kiss on film. Hopefully, they'll create an MTV Award for that category."

OPPOSITE: The ostrich race in full swing; ABOVE: Ostrich wranglers Jennifer Henderson and Bill Rivers tend to the birds on location in Bouaissoun.

RICHARD COYLE

TUS

It's not surprising that Richard Coyle zeroed in on his *Prince of Persia: The Sands of Time* character from the moment he first read the script. Coyle is an actor's actor, most admired by his fellow artists, equally adept at working on screen, onstage, or in television. And it takes a great deal of skill for an actor who projects as much strength and confidence as the handsome Coyle does to project so effectively a character ruled primarily by self-doubt.

"Tus is on a journey to listen to his heart and not just his head," observes Coyle in the ornate Alamut Palace set on Pinewood Studios' S stage. "My character's a politician, if you like, and he bears a great weight of responsibility. But he wears it very heavily, and his story is about learning to accept his destiny and be comfortable with it.

"Great men wear their greatness easily and effortlessly. I think that Tus has greatness in him, but he doesn't know how to wear it. He has to learn to become that person. He's very ambitious, very confused, and very keen to carry on the great traditions of Persia. That's a great thing as an actor to play, because Tus continues to grow throughout the film. Destiny is a general theme in this film. It seems to me that every character is plowing the same sort of paths in dealing with their destinies."

Born in Sheffield and educated at the University of York, Richard Coyle graduated from the prestigious Old Vic Theatre school in 1998, and only two years later was cast as Jeff Murdock in the hit British television series *Coupling*. Although the program made him a star in his native Britain, Coyle left the series to pursue roles onstage, and was cast alongside Gwyneth Paltrow in the Donmar Warehouse production of *Proof*. That role led to several other highly praised theater performances, as well as feature-film appearances in *The Libertine* (starring Johnny Depp) and Ridley Scott's *A Good Year*.

"I've never done anything this big before," notes Coyle of his work in *Prince of Persia*. "In fact, I don't know many people who have done something this size! It's astonishingly massive, and sometimes it amazes me, like the first time we saw the Alamut set in Morocco. It was as if they had resurrected a ruined ancient city. I walked around thinking, I'm here. I'm in the ancient world. It was extraordinary galloping down a hill with a real army behind me, not just five guys who were going to be replicated in CG. The noise of five hundred extras on horseback is pretty impressive. . . . And when you're riding at the head of five hundred people, it really helps you slip into character!"

TOBY KEBBELL
Garsiv

In Toby Kebbell's native British vernacular, *wicked* doesn't imply something nasty or evil, but rather very, very cool. And in that sense, one can turn the tricky adjective right back on the young actor from the north of England—he is very wicked indeed. Increasingly well known and respected in his own country for his performances in a series of fine independent British productions, including *Dead Man's Shoes*, *Control*, and Guy Ritchie's *RocknRolla*, Kebbell capped off 2008 by being nominated by the British Academy of Film and Television Arts (BAFTA) for a Rising Star Award. He had already won a British Independent Film Award as Best Supporting Actor for *Control*, as well as the Edinburgh Film Festival's Trailblazer Award. But now, with his important role in *Prince of Persia: The Sands of Time*, Kebbell is perched on the edge of a major-league breakout into the big time.

Born in North Yorkshire and raised in Nottinghamshire, Kebbell fell in love with acting while still in grade school. He was discovered by filmmaker Shane Meadows while attending the Central Television Workshop. After starring in the director's *Dead Man's Shoes*, Kebbell was cast by Oliver Stone in a small but pivotal role in *Alexander*, which resulted in the actor's first tour of duty in Morocco.

Kebbell's envelope-pushing performances brought him to the attention of Jerry Bruckheimer and Mike Newell, who thought him the perfect choice to portray the militaristic and unyielding Garsiv. Kebbell developed a clear-eyed interpretation of Garsiv, who chases Dastan relentlessly after he believes his adoptive brother was responsible for their father's assassination. "He's an absolute brute," admits Kebbell during a break in filming at Pinewood Studios, having survived months of shooting in the brute-al Moroccan heat. "What he lacks in skills he's made up for in brutality. And he understands the power of fear. Garsiv is a genuine, fire-blood prince, and he's pretty scary. He's the kind of guy at school who is a bit of a thug, the kind of dude who is happy to fight and causes a lot of hassles.

"After King Sharaman is assassinated and Dastan is pegged as the murderer, Garsiv has the perfect opportunity, as the head of the Persian army, to pursue his brother," Kebbell continues. "He's always seeking a mission, and his pursuit of Dastan gives him a purpose in life. But Garsiv is not without honor, which leads to a very surprising turn of events in the story."

Toby Kebbell is also clear on what attracted him to the role of Garsiv. "I love action movies. It's all very well being an actor who does art-house roles, but passion can come across in an action film, too. Good acting is good acting, no matter where it's placed. It was great to work and train hard, learn to ride a horse, fight with an ax, do stunts. I'm one of those actors who believe that we all put on a little bit of a performance anyway as human beings.

"The action stuff is ridiculously hard," Kebbell confesses, "like running up the side of a cliff at nine thousand feet above sea level. But it's like waiting in a queue for a roller coaster. You're sweating with nerves, and then when you get there, take the ride, and it's over, you say, 'Oh, man, let's have another go.'"

Which is, of course, *wicked*. Wicked enough, in fact, that Toby Kebbell followed his role in *Prince of Persia: The Sands of Time* by promptly signing up for another Jerry Bruckheimer film. He would go on to portray sinister illusionist Drake Stone in *The Sorcerer's Apprentice* opposite Nicolas Cage, Jay Baruchel, and Kebbell's fellow *Persia* cast member Alfred Molina.

STEVE TOUSSAINT
Seso

"Seso is the right-hand man and confidant of an outlaw leader called Sheikh Amar, who is played by a little-known actor by the name of Alfred Molina," says Steve Toussaint, tongue at least partly planted in cheek. "Seso is a member of the Ngbaka, an African tribe. He's an expert with knives and has an awful lot of them, including one wonderful throwing knife, which has three blades. When we first see Seso, we think he might be a little bit mean, but that's revealed to be the opposite by the end of the movie."

It soon became apparent to one and all on the *Prince of Persia* set that Steve Toussaint, with his acting skills and striking physicality, was born to portray Seso's courage, nobility, and loyalty. Born in England, Toussaint is a familiar presence on British television, having played recurring roles in such popular series as *The Knock*, *Doctors*, *My Dad's the Prime Minister*, *The Bill*, *Silent Witness*, and *Broken News*. More recently, the actor has begun crossing the pond to appear on such U.S. TV programs as Jerry Bruckheimer's *CSI: Miami*, in which he played Judge Hugo Kemp on three episodes.

Along with his fellow *Prince of Persia* cast members, Toussaint embarked on a rigorous training program. "One morning, four or five of us went to Hyde Park with Jake Gyllenhaal, and that was a real ego bash," he recalls with a laugh, "because Jake is extremely fit, and we weren't so much. But then I started combat training with the stunt team, and lots of knife training, which never really stopped. I got to work with two wonderful fight coordinators, Ben Cooke and Tom Dupont, who took me through a lot of general combat but also a lot of knife-throwing techniques."

Toussaint does note, though, that he had it somewhat easier than his costars in Morocco: "I was one of the lucky ones, because my African costume is quite revealing, as opposed to Fred

Molina, Toby Kebbell, and Richard Coyle, who were wearing layers of clothing or armor. Costume designer Penny Rose's idea was that Seso had basically collected his attire along the way, so there was a kind of deliberate mismatch. But his costume also had to be utilitarian. So, for example, he has leather trousers patched together from different bits, because he's riding through the desert a lot. Seso also has a leopard-skin covering, which I've been told is very sexy. You be the judge.

"In some ways, *Prince of Persia: The Sands of Time* is an old-fashioned adventure movie, but it has a lot more grit to it," concludes Toussaint. "It's a lot more hard-edged than anything I've seen in this genre, because there are real life-and-death issues in the story. There's comedy, romance, and wondrous special effects, but there are certain parallels with what's been happening in the world these past two or three years, and it would be nice if people picked up on that."

REECE RITCHIE
BIS

Reece Ritchie, a strikingly handsome, youthful but already accomplished actor, was selected to portray Prince Dastan's aide-de-camp. "Bis is a nobleman who has been appointed not exactly to watch over Dastan, but to make sure that he doesn't get into any compromising scrapes, or do anything too reckless," Ritchie explains, ". . . which he of course does . . . and Bis has to kind of tag along wiping the sweat off his brow.

"Bis is Dastan's right-hand man, and kind of his conscience," Ritchie adds. "Dastan has this rogue streak in his blood, and Bis is the one who has to say, 'Well, hang on, maybe that's not such a great idea.' He's constantly breaking a slow sweat just in case Dastan trips over something, says the wrong thing, is late, or isn't wearing the right clothing for these royal meetings. But Bis has a real loyalty to Dastan, so he would never wholeheartedly disagree with him, or try and prevent Dastan from doing what he wants."

When push comes to shove, though, Bis is right there beside Dastan in an advance commando raid on Alamut. "We're the elite force, the crème de la crème of the Persian army," Ritchie notes, "so I had to train for the role. Jake and I ran around Hyde Park a few times, and he said that every time we ran by a bench we had to either do twenty pushups or tricep dips. Once we got to the fifth bench, I jokingly said to Jake, 'I'm going to come back at midnight and unbolt a couple of these benches!'" Ritchie also did rigorous combat training along with the others in Morocco, under George Aguilar and his stunt team, and he did considerable horse training in Madrid with Ricardo Cruz Moral.

In fact, Ritchie did most of his own stunts and nearly all of the fighting on-screen. "I love doing stunts, and maybe it's my ego, but I don't want to sit in the cinema and say, 'Oh, that wasn't me.' I really wanted to get involved as much as I could, and both stunt coordinators, George Aguilar on first unit and Greg Powell on second unit, were very accommodating."

Having recently come from playing an important role in Peter Jackson's *The Lovely Bones*, Ritchie found himself having an opportunity to work with yet another of film's most distinguished directors, Mike Newell, on *Prince of Persia: The Sands of Time*. "Mike's very direct, which I like. You know straightaway what he's thinking, which makes me, as an actor, feel very relaxed," Ritchie says. "There's nothing worse than having to second-guess a director. Yet, the grandeur of what he's done before doesn't possess Mike as a director. He's still human and very approachable."

One aspect of the film that excited Ritchie was "the fact that it introduces audiences to the ancient Near East and tackles some of the issues that we're still dealing with, but it's still designed to entertain. I didn't have any preconceptions about the Middle East, and as a person of mixed race myself, I certainly don't draw on any generalizations."

Most of all, though, Reece Ritchie was thrilled with what his character was called upon to do on-screen. "We get into all sorts of adventures: The storming of Alamut, which is amazing; scaling walls, breaching gates, riding horses—all sorts of fun stuff. I'm burning with excitement."

King Sharaman

With his vast background playing every conceivable role on stage, screen, and television, the greatly respected British character actor Ronald Pickup was a natural choice to play King Sharaman. Jerry Bruckheimer and Mike Newell wanted to cast an actor who could infuse nobility and humanity into the monarch, who adopts a young street urchin named Dastan and makes him a Prince of Persia.

"What interested me about the role," says Pickup, "is that for all of his power—which is absolute—Sharaman has strange doubts and fears about what is kingship, what is leadership, and which of his sons will carry the torch. In a curious way, there's a kind of liberal streak to Sharaman, something that is beyond absolute and fierce power, and it's that kind of ambivalence that attracted me to the character.

"There's something almost irrational in Sharaman's decision to adopt Dastan when he's a boy," continues Pickup. "He has two wonderful sons, but one, Garsiv, is a bit bloodthirsty, and the other, Tus, is filled with self-questioning. He then encounters this little boy who is gutsy, and feisty, and, against all odds, commits an act of extraordinary bravery. *Prince of Persia: The Sands of Time* is about what is power, what is fatherhood, what is brotherhood, what is family, what is love?"

Along with the rest of the cast members, Pickup committed himself wholeheartedly to preparation for the film, including horse training in Madrid with equestrian Ricardo Cruz Moral. "We had a crash course for a week, and I didn't become a brilliant rider," the actor confesses self-deprecatingly. "But what was wonderful about the training was that, thanks to the

preparation we had, you just stopped worrying about it when you filmed."

And as for the fiery heat of the Moroccan summer, Pickup admits that "I didn't have it as bad as some, including the actors playing my sons—Jake, Toby, and Richard—who were constantly wearing armor and shooting fight scenes. I was just able to sit elegantly on a horse and be well treated by everyone. On some days, though, the set became a cauldron, so I did dive down off the horse and get a bottle of water now and then."

Whatever his equestrian skills, there seems to be little that Ronald Pickup hasn't accomplished in his distinguished forty-five-year career on stage, screen, and television. Since making his debut in 1964 with an episode during the very first season of the British television cult classic *Dr. Who*, Pickup has played roles that have included a bewildering number of real-life personages ranging from Lord Randolph Churchill to composers Igor Stravinsky and Giuseppe Verdi, philosopher Friedrich Nietzsche, and scientist Albert Einstein. Among his more than 100 screen and TV credits are his voice performances as Aslan in three late 1980s/early '90s BBC films: *The Chronicles of Narnia*: *The Lion, the Witch and the Wardrobe*, *The Voyage of the Dawn Treader*, and *The Silver Chair*. So Ronnie Pickup knows a thing or two about fantasy and its effect on audiences.

"I think that people will take away so much from *Prince of Persia: The Sands of Time*," he says. "It's a fantasy with characters everyone can relate to. It's also a thumping-good whodunit, a cracking adventure yarn, and a great love story. The movie is huge, but with lots of nuance and lovely grace notes and detail."

WILLIAM FOSTER
Young Dastan

There was no happier person on the set of *Prince of Persia: The Sands of Time* than the energetic, good-humored, handsome young William "Will" Foster, who portrays the leaping, jumping, and running young Dastan. And why not? He was living out his dreams. All eleven years' worth of them.

The athletic young native of Norwich, England, who had studied parkour for nine months, responded to a posting on a parkour Web site looking for an eleven-year-old boy with dark hair, blue eyes, and some proficiency in the discipline. "A week later, they asked if I wanted to come to Ealing Studios for a meeting, and then there was one more after that. And then they phoned my mom and told her that they wanted me in the movie."

Will Foster first discovered parkour when his math teacher went on vacation and was replaced by a substitute who turned out to be more interested in athletics than in adding and subtracting. "Instead of teaching us math, he showed us a documentary about parkour, and immediately afterwards we all ran into the playground and everyone started climbing and jumping."

Will had acted in only a few school plays, but was up to the physical conditioning that was required for the arduous work he would perform in both Ouarzazate, Morocco, and closer to home at Pinewood Studios in the United Kingdom. In the elaborate Nasaf set constructed at Kasbah Ait Ben Haddou, Will dangled from a roof, ran through the streets, climbed a building, jumped over obstacles, climbed over pots, and then had a challenging and dramatic scene with Ronald Pickup as King Sharaman and Sir Ben Kingsley as Nizam. "It's fun and hard work," says Will, "but the fun kind of takes over." Will loved his work, but also enjoyed hanging out with fellow child cast member Elliot James Neale, who played Dastan's friend Yusef.

Studying parkour was a natural progression for William Foster, it seemed. "It's given me a way to turn something that I had already been doing into a discipline. I've always been climbing on things ever since I was three years old. And parkour is just efficient movement, really: getting from A to B as quickly and fluidly as possible. It's been amazing," he continues. "It was really short notice flying to Morocco, and the sets are so cool. They've given me some props as souvenirs, including my Dastan's message pack."

Will was also thrilled by the opportunities of meeting not only his older counterpart, Jake Gyllenhaal, but also the very founder of parkour, David Belle—one of his heroes. "Will is a parkour fanatic," says Mike Newell, "and when he saw who was going to instruct him—this great French god, David Belle—his eyes popped."

Dreams can, it seems, come true after all.

GISLI ORN GARDARSSON
Zolm, Lead Hassansin

Actor, director, producer, writer, and gymnast, Gisli Orn Gardarsson is Iceland's surprise gift to the world of theater and film. Bursting beyond the confines of his island and a culture that manages to be simultaneously strongly traditional and fantastically avant-garde (as any fan of Sigur Rós and Björk can attest), Gardarsson has made considerable inroads into worldwide theatrical circles with his Reykjavik-based troupe Vesturport, which he cofounded. Vesturport's wildly imaginative, fresh, and irreverent productions of Shakespeare's *Romeo and Juliet*, Büchner's *Woyzeck*, Kafka's *Metamorphosis*, and other plays have been seen and praised in the United Kingdom, Germany, Russia, Korea, and Spain. Often starring in and directing the productions, Gardarsson has also produced and starred in several Icelandic films, often acting on both screen and stage with his wife, Nina Dogg Filupsdottir.

The energetic and good-natured Gardarsson, in startling contrast to the terrifying nature of the character he portrays in *Prince of Persia: The Sands of Time*, trained in gymnastics for fifteen years and was on Iceland's national team. Thus, he was able to meld together his theatrical and physical backgrounds for his role as Zolm, the Hassansin leader with cold, merciless, piercing eyes. But there was still much for him to learn.

"I had to do a lot of sword-fight training and filming, which is very different and a lot like choreography," he notes. "Because the Hassansins are trained assassins and there's nobody better than they at using weapons, it's essential that it becomes organic to your movements." The horsemanship necessary for his role came a little easier for Gardarsson. "I have horses in Iceland, although they're smaller than the ones we use in the film. They put me on quite an intensive training program with the horses in Madrid and Morocco, because when you're shooting a scene, there isn't room for any kind of uncertainty or insecurity."

Another challenge for Gardarsson was actually being able to see through the ice-blue contact lenses he was obliged to wear, although his own eyes are also a piercing Icelandic blue. "The lenses give the character a little bit something extra, you know. They're really eerie, there's something animalistic in them. But wearing them gives you tunnel vision, so doing all the fighting can be a bit scary when you can only see twenty percent of what you're accustomed to."

Despite the fact that his character is both lethal and heartless, Gisli Orn Gardarsson was compelled to find some connection that would allow him to play something more than just an emblem of faceless evil. "Icelandic people know their mythology, can read the sagas in the original language, and have a proud connection to the past. I think that the Hassansin ideals of fearlessness, dying in battle, and going to paradise are things every Icelander can recognize as being part of their ancestral history."

SEVEN HORSEMEN OF THE APOCALYPSE: THE HASSANSINS

Swathed from head to toe in black garb, armed with a terrifying array of weaponry, and focused on one thing—dealing death under orders—the Hassansins are the almost spectral warriors relentlessly pursuing the Dagger of Time, and, therefore, Dastan and Tamina. "The Hassansins were raised as children to become warriors and killers, and have absolutely no conscience," explains Jerry Bruckheimer. "They're almost mystical characters who can do unbelievable feats, practicing their dark craft since birth, so they're really formidable adversaries."

"We do in fact get our word *assassin* from 'Hassansin,'" says Mike Newell, referring to the militant sect active in the Middle East from the eighth to fourteenth centuries. "They were indeed based on real history, but in our story, they inhabit that borderland between reality and fantasy."

There are seven Hassansins bedeviling our heroes in *Prince of Persia: The Sands of Time*, each one with a lethal specialty. The leader, Zolm (Gisli Orn Gardarsson), releases vipers from his sleeves that then burrow at great speed underground to reach their prey. Hassad (Thomas Dupont) wields whips tipped with spiky blades and a catching claw. Ghazab (Domonkos Pardanyi) fights with a nasty, double-bladed Halberd. The appropriately named Gool (David Pope) has a giant scimitar that can slice through metal. Nefrat (Frudik Vladimir) throws orbs containing Greek fire, an early form of hand grenade. Tamah (Massimiliano Ubaldi) wears metal arm pieces that contain a spring-action blade and razor-sharp trident; and Setam (Claudio Pacifico) fires sharp metal spikes from arm plates, or flings them with brutal accuracy. All of the above weapons were specially fabricated by armorer Richard Hooper in workshops either in Marrakesh or at Pinewood Studios. Zolm's vipers, on the other hand, were totally in the domain of visual-effects supervisor Tom Wood.

"The Hassansins are my favorite characters in the movie," says Gemma Arterton (ironically, considering the fact that her character, Tamina, is their prime target), "because I just love the darkness they bring into the film. They're outcasts who have been raised as killing machines, and they're a mystery or legend." In fact, Arterton was obliged to fight off the Hassansins in a rip-roaring battle scene shot in the Atlas Mountains at Oukaimden. "That was the first week of filming, and it was mad," she recalls. "It was all quite calm and quiet, and then all of a sudden these Hassansins seem to just fall from the sky. It's really fierce. There's a shot in which the Hassansin leader, a killing machine, is coming towards Tamina, and it's really petrifying. I fight the Hassansins, which is a real feat in itself because they're experts. I think that really shows Tamina's bravery and courage. It was really weird . . . I suppose that's how it is in battle, where you focus on the one thing that you're doing, with all of these other fights happening around you. All you can think about is where the sword is, and why you've got to protect yourself. There must have been fifty or more stuntmen all doing their own battles, with dust everywhere. It was brilliant."

What make the Hassansins so terrifying? "Well, I guess it's living in a dark cellar with each other, bad company all around," quips Gisli Orn Gardarsson, who plays Zolm. "They just become emotionally numb. The Hassansins' mission is to find the Dagger of Time, so that is the goal. It's not about killing people . . . but whoever gets in the way will be taken out of the way."

"The Hassansins are actually very mystical," adds Thomas Dupont, the film's co-fight coordinator who also

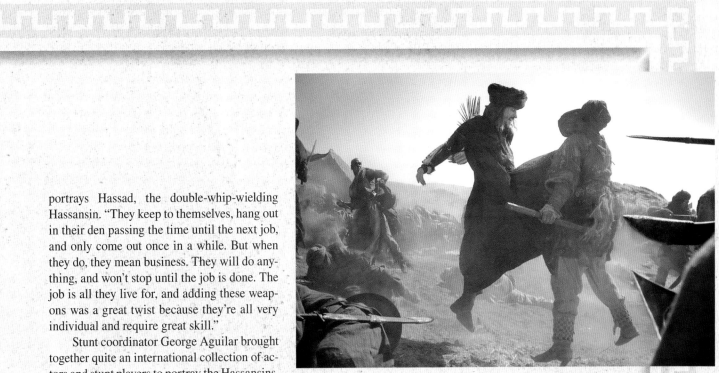

portrays Hassad, the double-whip-wielding Hassansin. "They keep to themselves, hang out in their den passing the time until the next job, and only come out once in a while. But when they do, they mean business. They will do anything, and won't stop until the job is done. The job is all they live for, and adding these weapons was a great twist because they're all very individual and require great skill."

Stunt coordinator George Aguilar brought together quite an international collection of actors and stunt players to portray the Hassansins. "We searched them out by their specialty," he explains. "Gisli Orn Gardarsson is from Iceland, and started out as a gymnast before turning to acting. Both Tom Dupont and David Pope are American. Tom is one of our co-fight coordinators, and David was an Olympic triathlete. Domonkos Pardanyi is Hungarian, Claudio Pacifico and Massimiliano Ubaldi are both Italian, and Frudik Vladimir is from Slovakia."

Tom Dupont is an old Jerry Bruckheimer Films hand by this point, having been a sword-fighting double for Geoffrey Rush, Bill Nighy, and Jack Davenport on all three Pirates of the Caribbean epics. But *Prince of Persia: The Sands of Time* represented a new challenge: to become an expert with double whips, one with razor-sharp blades and the other with a metal claw for grasping. "Double whips are quite intricate in themselves, and putting weapons on the ends of them adds yet another dimension," says Dupont. "There was a lot of rehearsal in learning how the whips were going to perform."

The work was never easy for the stuntmen portraying these seven horsemen of the Apocalypse, starting with their training on the football field of the Kawkab Training Pitch in Marrakesh. "The heat was incredible, and we were just starting our massive rehearsals for the Hidden Valley fight sequence with the Hassansins," recalls Dupont. "There were only seven of us, fighting like seventy, choreographing a lot of different moves for the Hassansins with our different weapons. It wasn't easy in itself, but when you add the heat, it was combustible. We went through a lot of water, and had to take breaks because we couldn't get through the whole day without stopping. We were really tested. The heat was tough, but we got through it because we all had a common goal: to make a great project."

LEFT and RIGHT: Concept illustrations of four Hassansins and their lethal weaponry; ABOVE: Setam (Claudio Pacifico) in battle against the Persian army in the Hidden Valley.

DAUD SHAH
Asoka

It's been a strange and wonderful journey for the handsome, athletic Daud Shah, who transitioned from the hospital to the battlefields of Alamut for *Prince of Persia: The Sands of Time*, rather than the other way around. Previously a practicing physician in London, Shah made a career switch, from medicine to the big screen, heeding a nagging passion that wouldn't let him be. In the film, Shah portrays the proud and loyal warrior Asoka, personal bodyguard to Tamina, who asks him to protect the Dagger of Time, imperiling his life, when Alamut is attacked by the Persians. There was peril indeed, as the ferocity of the fight scene between Asoka and Dastan—who is unaware of what is being protected until he discovers the Dagger after defeating Asoka—was intense enough potentially to land both actors in the hospital!

Ironically, when Shah started acting a few years ago, "I went to a talk because Mike Newell was going to speak about his experiences of being a director. I just thought, 'This is a guy I'd love to work with.' So when I finally met Mike to audition for this part, I really felt like I was living a dream."

Like so many others in the cast, Shah trained hard for his role and was glad to be reunited with fight coordinator Ben Cooke, with whom he had previously worked on *Casino Royale* (Shah engaged in furious fisticuffs with Daniel Craig's 007 in the brutal opening sequence of the film). "George Aguilar, Ben, and the others are an amazingly professional team. I did a lot of stage combat at drama school, learning five different weapons, and then learned hand-to-hand combat for *Casino Royale*. I've always enjoyed the physical aspect of acting. It's a great way of getting into character, and even if it's a small part in a film where there's little or no action, it all starts with how the character moves."

Daud Shah, born of an English mother and a father with Afghan and Kashmiri roots, is proud that *Prince of Persia: The Sands of Time* "helps to bring back an alternative view of the Near East. It's wonderful to see that part of the world being portrayed in a way that is so different from the unfortunate events of the recent past."

Long-Legged (and Short-Legged) Beasties

The set of *Prince of Persia: The Sands of Time* was a great place to be for an animal lover. But woe and sad tidings to any individual not enamored of myriad beasties furred or feathered, as the film was absolutely packed with them, from Marrakesh and throughout Morocco all the way back to Pinewood Studios outside of London.

"We've got a lot of varied animals on this film," noted veteran animal coordinator Gill Raddings. Outside the pens on the dusty outskirts of the giant Alamut set in the Moroccan village of Tamesloht, the rich smell of droppings weighed heavily upon one's nostrils. "Of course, we have camels, about twenty of them, trained to be ridden and to carry packs," Raddings says. "They look terrific and are bigger than people realize, so when you have big spaces to fill on set, they're great for that." Raddings insisted that camels have gotten a bad rap for their perceived ill temper, their bouts of spitting, and other antisocial behavior: "They can be stubborn, they can be a bit moody, but it's more the perception and the sounds they make. They're not being grumpy—it's just what they sound like. The camels on set are wonderful. They don't kick, they don't spit, they don't bite, and they don't spook at anything. With a battle raging around them, the camels just stand there, chewing their cud and looking down their long noses at everyone and everything."

Of course, there was that one unexpected dromedarian incident during a beastly hot day of filming in Agafay during which the scene of the Persian army approaching Alamut was shot. "They can get a little moody when they've decided they've had enough," says Raddings. "One of the camels managed to dump its rider and then go for a flat-out gallop across the desert in the opposite direction, with a lot of us hurrying after it on quad bikes. But once he had his exercise, he came back and carried on filming. He just wanted his little moment, which just goes to prove that if an animal wants to do something, he's going to do it. You just have to go with the flow sometimes, just like you do with human actors."

"Then, of course, we have lots of sheep and goats," adds Raddings. "We put the actual shepherds into costume, so that they could continue to take care of their flocks. We also have plenty of mules and donkeys, which are used for both work and transportation all over Morocco." Not to mention ravens, crows, chickens, lions, deer, and at least twenty snakes (including a gigantic Burmese python).

There were also two ornately plumed peacocks, used for the Alamut scenes in Morocco, and numerous brilliantly colored exotic birds—chattering lorikeets, blue and gold macaws, parrots, fancy pigeons, and a huge toucan—used in the Alamut garden set on S Stage at Pinewood Studios. The birds were happy to sing a medley of their greatest hits when least expected, and avian coordinator Anthony Bloom warned that a couple of them could talk a blue streak when they had a mind to. "One bird has a vocabulary of colorful swearwords, and another, named Peppy, speaks soliloquies in a thick Scottish accent," advised Bloom. "I just hope they don't start talking during Jake Gyllenhaal and Gemma Arterton's dialogue."

Clearly, for any film set in the ancient Near East that involves large-scale battles, horses were essential. Heading the equestrian department was notable horse master Ricardo Cruz Moral, who brought some twenty magnificent beasts from Madrid to Morocco. Included among them were the marvelously noble, stalwart Friesians, who "portrayed" Aksh, the prized horse Dastan steals from his brother Garsiv while escaping from Alamut. Cruz Moral and his team not only took care of the horses, but also trained the primary cast of the film in Spain before filming got under way. Some sixty additional horses were added from Moroccan stables.

Gill Raddings also had several dogs—more, in fact, than were required, because she was actively working with the local Moroccan rescue center, Spana. "They have rescue units all over Africa and do marvelous work," beams Raddings. "I've trained six dogs from the rescue center, some of which have already been on camera. And at the end of the film, we're going to find them all really good homes."

Of course, hosting such a plethora of non-toilet-trained beasts made it difficult for the company members to avoid various and sundry steaming piles of fresh animal waste (although after enough time in the desert, one tended to plow right on through, whatever the consequences).

sailing the sea of sand

HISTORY AND FANTASY

Screenwriters Carlo Bernard and Doug Miro, both looking suitably awestruck, walk through the massive exterior set representing the city of Alamut, which has been constructed within the ancient walls of the Moroccan village of Tamesloht. Although just a twenty-kilometer drive southwest of Marrakesh, a detour off the road to the mellifluously named Amizmiz, Tamesloht is a dusty, unpaved village consisting of not much more than a few shops, some exceedingly humble dwellings, a gendarme station, friendly townspeople, and walls of an ancient kasbah reputed to be some 700 years old. Rising from the dusty Moroccan earth is a surreal vision of an imaginary city: a magnificent square, with a white-and-gold, Taj Mahal-like palace rising fifty feet above the ground; an adjacent, elegant, red-and-white structure festooned with balconies; and a central fountain spouting water, flanked by elephant statues ranging in size from diminutive to, well, elephantine. Streets abound with architectural and decorative detail: scroll shops in a narrow alley bedecked by small, tinkling bells; a gorgeous,

pale-yellow temple adorned with garlands of vividly colored flowers; arches carved with floral designs in bas relief; stalls selling shoes, dried herbs, and flowers; ancient mud walls festooned with imaginative frescoes of men and beasts; and a number of statues and shrines. "There aren't many sets," says Carlo Bernard, "that are so big you can actually get *lost* in them!"

This is Alamut, as designed by *Prince of Persia: The Sands of Time* production designer Wolf Kroeger. In scale and detail, it recalls the golden age of the cinematic epic: Cecil B. DeMille's *The Ten Commandments*, William Wyler's *Ben-Hur,* Anthony Mann's *The Fall of the Roman Empire* and *El Cid,* and other spectacles that preceded the digital age.

But Jerry Bruckheimer is a man who believes that tradition and innovation are not mutually exclusive, so he, director Mike Newell, and designer Kroeger set forth to create, in three dimensions, sets of extraordinary scope and depth. These sets would later be digitally extended under visual-effects supervisor Tom Wood.

"Wolf Kroeger is a real artist," says Jerry Bruckheimer of the man selected to design the physical world of *Prince of Persia: The Sands of Time*. "He has great vision, amazing attention to detail, and isn't afraid to think big and build big."

Mike Newell agrees: "Wolf has a wonderful ability to tune himself. He's fantastic with two things: one is the big overall concept,

and the other is expressing the concept through minute detail. He has a painterly eye, and, like myself, he was inspired by Orientalist art. But Wolf also did an enormous amount of research into ancient Persian and Near Eastern architecture. We spent days and days looking at pictures of Iran. We would have loved to shoot there, but that was obviously impossible.

"Wolf gathers baskets of little details," continues Newell, "but then you realize that you're dealing with a man who re-created the birth of America in *The Last of the Mohicans* and rebuilt Stalingrad for *Enemy at the Gates*. There's actually nothing that Wolf can't do, because he jumps completely into the drama of the thing, and then he'll chew away at it like some mad terrier. It's sometimes hell being alongside him while he's doing this, but it's a really impressive process."

OPPOSITE: Spectacular visual effects overview of Alamut, with the imposing gold-domed palace as its centerpiece; ABOVE: A temple under construction in the huge Alamut exterior set; LEFT: Production designer Wolf Kroeger in front of his Alamut Palace.

*Wolf Kroeger is a real artist. He has great vision, amazing
attention to detail, and isn't afraid to think big and build big.*

—Jerry Bruckheimer

Wolf Kroeger's creations for *Prince of Persia: The Sands of Time* weren't just sets, but complete environments that enveloped the cast and created an alternate world that combined history and fantasy with truly unleashed imagination. Working to ensure that Kroeger's creations would make as smooth a journey into three dimensions as possible were supervising art director Jonathan McKinstry (for Morocco), supervising art director Gary Freeman (U.K.), set decorator Elli Griff, prop master David Balfour, armorer Richard Hooper, construction supervisors John Maher (Morocco) and Brian Neighbour (U.K.), and an entire army of artists and technicians (in the final unit list for the film, art department personnel take up seven full pages of small-print names). Work on the film's design began months before the cameras were switched on. A battery of art directors, set designers, conceptual illustrators, storyboard artists, and researchers mined the depths of their imaginations to develop the world envisioned by Bruckheimer, Newell, and Kroeger.

The version of pre-Islamic, sixth-century Persia created by Kroeger and his cohorts comes from a deliberate attempt to interweave authentic architecture and meticulously researched design elements with a high degree of fantasy, as dictated by the fanciful and supernatural element in the story. Alamut is entirely fictitious, a kind of Shangri-la, with a noticeable Indian influence. "From a design point of view," notes Jonathan McKinstry, "the sets, set dressing, and props are historical-looking pieces. However, because we're not making a factual historical film, we haven't locked ourselves into any one particular style. And since we are relying on a lot of Moroccan locations, there's admittedly some North African flavor in the designs as well."

"Jerry, Mike, and Wolf wanted designs unique in their scale and character, with a real epic feel," notes Gary Freeman. "Also, to make them rustic and rough, and not too clean-cut, but to have a real edge to them."

"It's a whole mélange of different cultures and styles," adds set decorator Elli Griff, "based on the Persian ornament. Then, for the designs of Alamut, it's the complete antithesis of Persia, with soft, ethereal colors and an Indian influence."

It was absolutely crucial for the various design departments to work together to synthesize their creations in a real harmonic convergence of artistry, but as Elli Griff points out, with everyone working at 125 percent of capacity, it wasn't easy: "The most important thing for any head of department was to be open and approachable for any other departments. A lot of the time, in all honesty, everyone is so busy with their own designs and manufacturing. But Penny Rose, the costume designer, was incredibly helpful and cooperative and, just in terms of inspiration, really generous. And if we have anything that will help another department, I always let it go because ultimately we are a team, and it's a global artistic effort."

Every design department would rely heavily on the extraordinary skills of Moroccan artisans, craftsmen, and builders. Nearly every single piece required by Elli Griff's set-decorating team, David Balfour's prop department, and Richard Hooper's armory crew was made especially for *Prince of Persia: The Sands of Time* in massive workshops in the Marrakesh industrial zone. Anything on wheels or carried by hand, including King Sharaman's astoundingly ornate horse-drawn hearse or the overweight Mughal's palanquin, was created and constructed by Stuart Rose, a specialist in that field. "Visiting the set-decoration and props warehouses was one of the most amazing experiences

I've had on any location of any of our movies," recalls Chad Oman, executive producer of Jerry Bruckheimer Films. "There were gigantic warehouses filled floor to ceiling with props and production-design elements, from lamps to swords to saddles for horses to all sorts of elaborate weaponry . . . all of it made right there, on the spot, by hand, by local artisans. There was one group forging swords, then another group hand-engraving the most minute detail on the swords. Around the corner were a group of men with little hammers creating brass lamps, another man handcrafting blankets for the horses, and someone else making the leather water bottle that Dastan and Tamina carry through the desert. It took five weeks of constant work to make that one bag, with elaborate stitching and beadwork. Really, I can't think of any other place in the world where you can get this kind of craftsmanship and artistry, and do it on a budget that's affordable."

All of the backbreaking, meticulous work, both in Morocco and the United Kingdom, was both acknowledged and appreciated by a grateful cast of performers. "When we went to Morocco," recalls Gemma Arterton, "in the first week we visited some of the sets that had been built, and that was when I realized, Whoa, this is a big deal. They were like cities. I'd never seen anything like it, and you do feel like you don't have to imagine anything. It's right there, and it's a real luxury, especially in these times of green screen. It was creating a world that really interested me in doing this film, and when you walk onto sets like ours, that world has already been created."

"Everywhere our eyes looked, we saw the most exquisitely carved walls, drapes, ramparts," added Sir Ben Kingsley toward the end of the film's shoot at Pinewood Studios. "And in Morocco, nature itself, the camels, thousands of horsemen, the dust. Our sets are so detailed that even if you're pausing, like I am,

halfway in a line and just breathing in, the amount of energy and information you're breathing in is extraordinary. Hours and hours of work have gone into this environment for you to act it. It's really uplifting, and it honored our craft to such a degree."

"*Prince of Persia: The Sands of Time* is something of an ancient road movie," notes Morocco supervising art director Jonathan McKinstry, "so we had to find a range of landscapes throughout the country to convey that progression." Working on the film in Morocco was also something of a road trip for the cast and crew, with a journey beginning in Marrakesh that wended its way overland first to Ouarzazate, and finally to the remote desert community of Erfoud. Along the way, Kroeger and company designed and built some remarkable sets on locations notable either for their unique physical characteristics, extant architecture, or both.

OPPOSITE: Rendering of colorful fresco paintings in Alamut;
ABOVE: Conceptual painting of the Alamut Palace interior; RIGHT:
the Nasaf Palace throne room constructed at Pinewood Studios.

MOROCCO
THE EXTERIOR SETS

Alamut

The Alamut set is something like five times the size of the 007 Stage at Pinewood Studios, and the palace courtyard alone is about one hundred meters by eighty meters," notes Jonathan McKinstry. "It was slightly scary to tackle such a monumental set with the time issue, but I always felt we could do it as long as we weren't held up with weather or other issues. It was a real photo finish. I think we were still finishing bits and pieces as the camera was turning over. From leveling the site and getting bulldozers in to the

camera rolling was just around fourteen weeks, so that's a lot in a little. We had a whole mold shop making carved decorations, panels, arches, for weeks and weeks. Most of Alamut was built using wood, plaster, and scaffolding, but for the mud walls we used scaffolding with a wooden frame, then mud dabs straight onto all of that to blend into the existing mud architecture of Tamesloht that we built around, so the mud naturally took on the color of the town itself. It naturally cracked like real mud does when it dries out.

"For the Indian-influenced architecture of Alamut," McKinstry continues, "we went with traditional plastic molds, timber frame, and plywood. An Italian sculptor carved the elephants for us, which are in the palace square, and a couple of English sculptors were in Morocco making all of the leaf work and molds for the carved decorations. The plaster shop made some-

ABOVE: Epic concept illustration of Alamut, with the Sky Chamber looming above the city; RIGHT: Filming at the huge Alamut Palace exterior set in Tamesloht, which was considerably expanded in the final version through digital extensions.

thing like two hundred giant brackets. And the colorful frescoes and murals were painted in seven weeks by scenic painter Roy Monk."

The monumental task of building Alamut, and all of the other sets for *Prince of Persia: The Sands of Time* in Morocco, was on the shoulders of John Maher. "For Alamut, we hired thirty miles of scaffolding tube and four hundred tons of plaster, which was molded, shaped, and sculpted," he notes. "We had lorry loads of timber from the U.K., and about three hundred and fifty people working, between the set and the workshop. We wore out a lot of work gloves, and the hard-hat restrictions were pretty tough. But, you know, our guys persevered, drank a lot of water, and got through it."

Set decorator Elli Griff admits that she had a field day adorning Alamut with her unique touch. "Alamut was a lovely set to dress. We sent some buyers off to India who came back with specific things that we couldn't possibly get where we were in Morocco. In the 'Scribe's Alley' we used lots of bells, because they're a sign of good luck and longevity. Then we go around the corner to the flower market, and that was all about color, getting these fabulous greens and turquoises against ocher backgrounds. For the courtyard in which Dastan fights with Asoka for possession of the Dagger of Time, the greens department brought in a beautiful old olive tree, which gave us a beautiful canopy to work with. Then we had different shrines made, adorned with sacrificial objects and flower petals."

TOP: Concept artist's atmospheric rendering of the streets of Alamut; BELOW: Completed version of Alamut temple, shown under construction on page 85; RIGHT: Dastan (Jake Gyllenhaal) discovers the Dagger of Time during the Persian assault on Alamut.

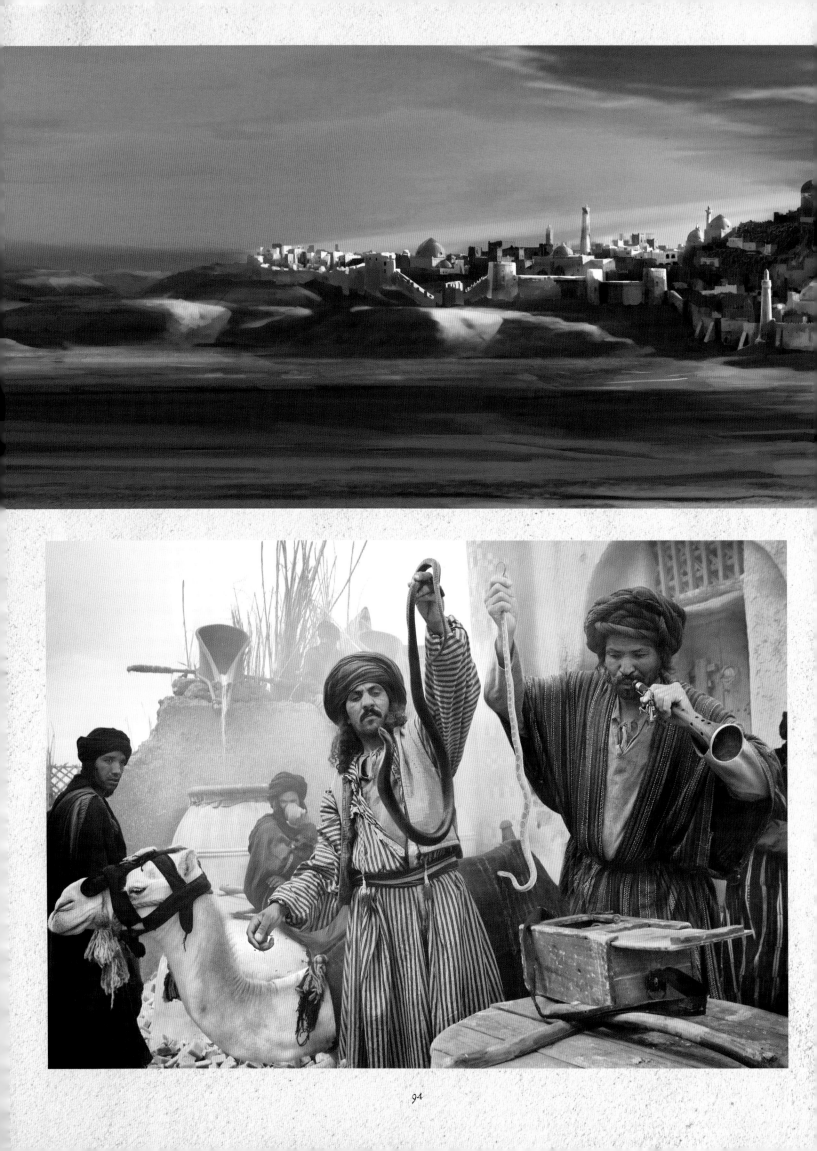

Nasaf Marketplace

Wolf Kroeger's expansive Nasaf marketplace, another huge exterior set, more closely resembled traditional Persian architecture. The marketplace featured huge gates with turquoise tiled domes, dye pits similar to those seen in the old Fez medina in Morocco, baking ovens, and shops selling rugs, leather, ceramic jars, baskets, and fruit—all provided by set decorator Elli Griff.

"Ait Ben Haddou is an ancient ksar about half an hour outside of Ouarzazate, and we built the Nasaf marketplace set just adjacent to it," explains Jonathan McKinstry. "Since it's a UNESCO World Heritage Site, we obviously couldn't shoot in the town itself, so we found an open area to the side where we built a composite of the marketplace and the entrance to the Persian royal palace. Lots of mud, split bamboo, and wooden-frame technology were used again, with lots of painted tiles. It took approximately twelve weeks to build the marketplace, from start to finish." The Nasaf set would utilize the structures of Ait Ben Haddou as part of its panoramic backdrop, with extensive digital renovations made by Tom Wood's visual-effects department.

sheikh Amar's ostrich Racetrack

W e see a lot of Wolf Kroeger's impish and dry sense of humor in Sheikh Amar's ostrich racetrack," notes Jonathan McKinstry of the ricky-ticky-tacky wooden racetrack—complete with owner's box—that Sheikh Amar (Alfred Molina) has constructed in his deliciously shabby desert fiefdom. "The set grew out of the fact that ostriches require an awful lot of penning in, because they're pretty dangerous birds and can get out. We had a specification from the ostrich handlers of not having any gap bigger than four inches. We were in a pretty spiky, rocky landscape at Bouaissoun, so we went with the idea of a spiky, post-type fencing that was consistent with what surrounded it."

In decorating the racetrack and owner's box, Elli Griff was able to utilize her own dry sense of humor. "The whole premise for me was that Sheikh Amar and his men had decorated the owner's box with things they had purloined and stolen from various villas and noblemen, both pretentious and a little rough," she says. "Then, believe it or not, I came across hundreds of ostrich eggs and thought that we should color them and hang them from the owner's box as decoration . . . and then let the wind take them and smash them against each other until there were just shards hanging."

Nasaf and Avrat streets and rooftops

Another ancient Moroccan dwelling was utilized by both the first and second units of the film to re-create sections of the Persian cities of Nasaf and Avrat: Kasbah Taourirte, in the heart of Ouarzazate. "We used it for the Avrat rooftops, almost exactly as is, with us adding a few bits and pieces," explains Jonathan McKinstry. "But we also used it for the back lanes and alleyways of Nasaf." So unspoiled was much of the kasbah's pise (mud and rubble) structure that Wolf Kroeger and his art department needed only to add some Persian domes and, for the extensive stunt work and parkour done across the length and breadth of its perilous rooftops, platforms and walls that had to blend in with the architecture.

The HIdden Valley

In building the environment of the Hidden Valley, Wolf Kroeger, Jonathan McKinstry, and their departments were able to make use of numerous extant Berber shepherds' huts in Oukaimden. "We did, however, create our 'hero' farmhouse—where Dastan battles Hassad, the Hassansin with the bladed whips—using local stone," notes McKinstry. "And we used local laborers to build that so it was totally consistent with all of the other structures that were there. It also had to fulfill a number of requirements from the stunt department for the action that takes place inside and on top of it."

"I wanted the Hidden Valley to have a really soft natural contrast to the detailed, embroidered, and ornate other sets," notes set decorator Elli Griff. "All of the dressing was very vernacular, all terra-cotta and earth—very basic."

PINEWOOD
The Studio Sets

outside inside

While the company was busy filming in Morocco, another team of art and construction personnel were frantically readying some thirty-five huge and complex sets on nine soundstages at Pinewood Studios back in the United Kingdom. "At one point we had a crew of one hundred and seventy," says U.K. supervising art director Gary Freeman. "I mean, at one point nearly one hundred plasterers were at work." During the preparation, Freeman was traveling from London to Morocco every other week to update Mike Newell and production designer Wolf Kroeger on the progress of the builds. In the hot seat was veteran construction manager Brian Neighbour. "Time really is the main factor," he confessed on the massive Alamut Eastern Gate set, while it was still under construction. "We have to bear in mind the rental cost of the stages. So, it's a tight schedule, and hard to complete on time. I was very lucky to be able to pick some great carpenters, plasterers, and painters."

The sheer amount of work and detail that went into the sets at Pinewood matched the Morocco builds at every turn. Says Gary Freeman, "Our head plasterer, Ken Barley, has been in this business for forty years and has worked on some huge movies, but when he tells me that *Prince of Persia: The Sands of Time* has the most complicated sets he's ever worked on, I believe him!"

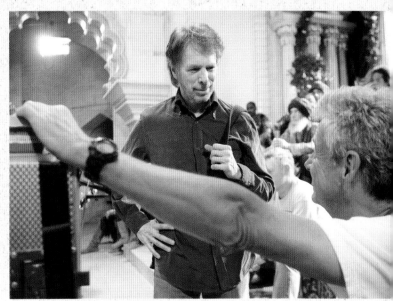

ABOVE: Just one portion of production designer Wolf Kroeger's Alamut Eastern Gate set on Pinewood Studios' massive "007 Stage"; RIGHT: Jerry Bruckheimer consults with director of photography John Seale on the Alamut Palace interior set on Pinewood Studios' S Stage.

Eastern Gate of Alamut

The jaw-dropping Eastern Gate of Alamut—with walls nearly fifty feet in height—occupied nearly the entire length, breadth, and height of the elephantine 007 Stage at Pinewood. Palm trees were imported from southern Spain and then carefully maintained by greensman Jon Marson and his team. The set was large enough for the filming of a massive battle scene involving hundreds of extras and twenty-five horses charging through gates and fire barriers. "The primary reason for building this set was night work involving lots of parkour and other stunt work, which would have been difficult to shoot in Morocco," says Freeman. U.K. construction manager Brian Neighbour built the Alamut Eastern Gate complex in an astonishingly short fourteen weeks. The gargantuan project required 3,000 eight-by-four-foot sheets of wood, 70,000 feet of three-by-one-inch timber, as well as forty tons of casting plaster for the moldings.

Alamut Palace Interior

The Alamut Great Hall, built on S Stage, was a lustrous amalgamation of Indian styles. Designed in cream tones with flecks of gold, the set featured arched ceilings, an overhanging canopy, and candelabras shaped like elephants. "I didn't want to use candlelight for this set," says set decorator Elli Griff. "I was determined to use only oil light, which turned out to be a bit of a feat. But John Seale, our cinematographer, felt that he got interesting light out of it. I've tried to use jeweled colors, low-level dressing, canopies, and things of that nature, which could bounce light."

The versatile Alamut Palace interior served as the foundation for several environments, including Tamina's throne room, Tus's chambers, and the banquet hall. "I wanted to make the base of Tamina's throne a crystal lotus flower, which subconsciously links to the crystalline Sandglass of the Gods," says Griff. "She has a huge, golden canopy above her throne with a hole in it so that the light can come down as if she has a direct connection with the gods and heaven. Everything about Tamina and her culture is accepting, soft, and humorous."

Tamina's chambers

A sumptuous fantasia of color, Tamina's chamber was a bedroom truly befitting a princess. Its walls were ornamented to resemble ancient illuminated manuscripts inlaid with precious jewels, and the peacock bed gave the room a plush, regal tone. "Mike and Wolf had a discussion in which they decided that Tamina's boudoir needed to be a fantastic, very feminine space," says Freeman.

"You have to do something that just begs disbelief, that's surreal and opulent," offers Elli Griff. "Tamina's bedroom is very jewel-encrusted, so that the low-level lights would cast an enchanted glow."

Alamut sky chamber

The Sky Chamber is the sanctum sanctorum, an aerie high above Alamut where the sacred Dagger of Time is kept. With its lustrously carved wooden statuary and stone pillars—all of the figures were hand-carved, then molded and cast—it has a temple-like feeling, which was accentuated during filming. Cinematographer John Seale's artfully projected shafts of light illuminated the magical dagger and bathed the ornate set in a spiritual glow, which was then enhanced by the lovely fragrance of burning incense. "If only this movie could be shown in Aromarama," quipped one crew member, recalling the late 1950s cinematic novelty in which odors were wafted to the audience through air-conditioning vents. "It's meant to be a very ancient part of the city," notes Gary Freeman, "and slightly weathered, because it's partially open to the elements."

Alamut Temple Garden

The Temple Garden was conceived as an idyllic slice of paradise, with exotic birds (lorikeets, macaws, parrots, toucans) in ornate cages; topiary elephants; a working fountain decorated with colorful statues of unicorns, rams, and peacocks; and an arch with jewel-encrusted frescoes. The trees were adorned with pale, translucent leaves—each one meticulously applied by hand—and golden lanterns and small tinkling bells. And the ground was strewn with red and yellow flower petals. "Wolf wanted to steer away from a purely realistic period garden," notes Gary Freeman. "Since it's for one of the most important scenes of the movie, he wanted to make it kind of a magic garden, using several Russian expressionist artists for inspiration."

Temple of Water

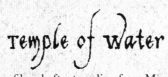

This magical set, the first in which the company filmed after traveling from Morocco to England, represents the sacred spot where the Dagger of Time is first found—and to which it must be returned. With waterfalls spilling into a pool and a shrine bedecked with treasures and spiritual offerings, the Temple of Water was a highly atmospheric environment, which enabled the company to reimmerse themselves in the *Prince of Persia* universe. Despite being constructed hundreds of miles from Morocco, the set had to tangentially match exteriors shot in Oukaimden. "Wolf was adamant that he wanted a big pool in a cave with a single light source coming in from above," explains Freeman. "We needed to match the color and texture of the Moroccan location, so we took a rock sample in Oukaimden and made a mold. Building a pool inside of a soundstage is always a nightmare. When you're in a closed environment, the last thing you want is thousands of gallons of water. So we used a company that did a great job for us, creating a hard surface that was fully waterproofed and super tough, and also worked well for the stunt fighting that had to take place in the pool."

Avrat Bazaar

This marvelous interior set was redolent of the exoticism of the ancient Persian world, replete with extensive set dressing that included everything from colorful carpets to ceremonially wrapped corpses. "Wolf did a sketch of the set, and then we built a model," explains Gary Freeman. "We knew from day one that there was a key action sequence that needed to be filmed on this set featuring lots of parkour, so Wolf wanted to create a series of vertical and horizontal structures that could contain the acrobatics. We took a team of plasterers to Morocco to get the textures as true as possible, and they took molds for the wall finishes. The real difficulty was in reinforcing the walls for the stunt players, so there's lots of metal hiding beneath the earthen structures."

Avrat streets and Rooftops

This expansive set on Pinewood's D Stage was a close match for scenes shot in Kasbah Taourirte in Ouarzazate, Morocco. The indoor incarnation of Avrat was built with earthen pisé structures and would serve as the stage for large segments of a major action sequence. A highlight of the scene is a stunt in which an entire Bedouin tent collapses to the ground from one of the rooftops, taking several Persian soldiers with it. For many of the crew, the set jolted them right back into Morocco, especially since the set had to be brightly lit to imitate sunshine. Because of the copious lighting, temperatures on the set rose to nearly North African levels.

PREVIOUS SPREAD: Tamina walks through the crowded alleyways of the remarkably detailed Avrat Bazaar set constructed at Pinewood Studios' A Stage; ABOVE and RIGHT: Jordan Mechner examines the architectural details of the Avrat Streets and Rooftops set on Pinewood's D Stage, with the huge lighting grid looming above.

Nasaf Palace and Throne Room

We took a lot of influences from Morocco as well as Persia for the Nasaf palace interior," says Gary Freeman. "We had a lot of the sculpture done there, because there's a sort of beautiful naïveté to their work. It's very intricate—perfect, but not too perfect. Sometimes there's a tendency to make everything too clean, whereas there's a certain subtle lightness to the handmade work that comes from Morocco. Obviously, it's incredibly decorative, with the zellige tile work that's so famous in Morocco and other parts of the Middle Eastern world. The designs are more geometric, whereas the Alamutian architecture is more curvaceous and has a more organic feel."

Den of the Hassansins

Wolf Kroeger discovered this great building near Ouarzazate," explains Freeman, "with a very ancient quality to it, very primitive pisé brickwork and finish. Wolf and Mike Newell loved the feel and size of it, so they shot the exterior in Morocco, and we created our version of the interior on B Stage at Pinewood. Wolf wanted it to feel like it was very deep, very dark, and very unwelcoming . . . unless you're one of the Hassansins."

The Sandroom

Unlike the vast majority of the sets, which were fully fabricated environments unto themselves, the Alamut substructure pieces constructed at Pinewood, including the massive Sand Chamber, were basic foundations that would later be enhanced by Tom Wood's visual-effects department. "We built the key elements that the actors and stunt players come into contact with," explains Freeman. "They're still quite large builds, because we have several challenges that Dastan and Tamina have to overcome before reaching the Sandglass of the Gods. It's a big collaboration between ourselves, Trevor Wood's special physical-effects department, and Tom Wood's visual-effects group. And although we're building just a microcosm of the set, some of the pieces are as large as thirty feet high and forty feet across."

sandglass of the gods

"The Sandglass is actually a large set piece shot against green screen," notes Gary Freeman. "Mike Newell wanted to shoot as much in camera as possible, so we tried to build as much as we could. The scene was cleverly pre-visualized by the visual-effects department." The Sandglass of the Gods was constructed of plaster, styrene, and urethane. "We built a large maquette model of it to different scales," Freeman explains, "so that Mike and director of photography John Seale could plan their camera angles."

Although Tom Wood's visual effects would ultimately give the Sandglass of the Gods its full visual impact, the filming of the climactic showdown between Dastan and Nizam certainly had an apocalyptic atmosphere. Plumes of smoke swirled from huge, roaring fans; blinding lightning and psychedelic streaks of color and light flashed throughout the set; and two huge, swooping camera cranes captured the action. It felt as if the fate of mankind truly hung in the balance.

ABOVE and BELOW: Filming the epic Sandglass of the Gods confrontation with Technocranes and green screens inside of Pinewood Studios' E Stage; RIGHT: Concept illustrations of Nizam's descent into the subterranean world of Alamut.

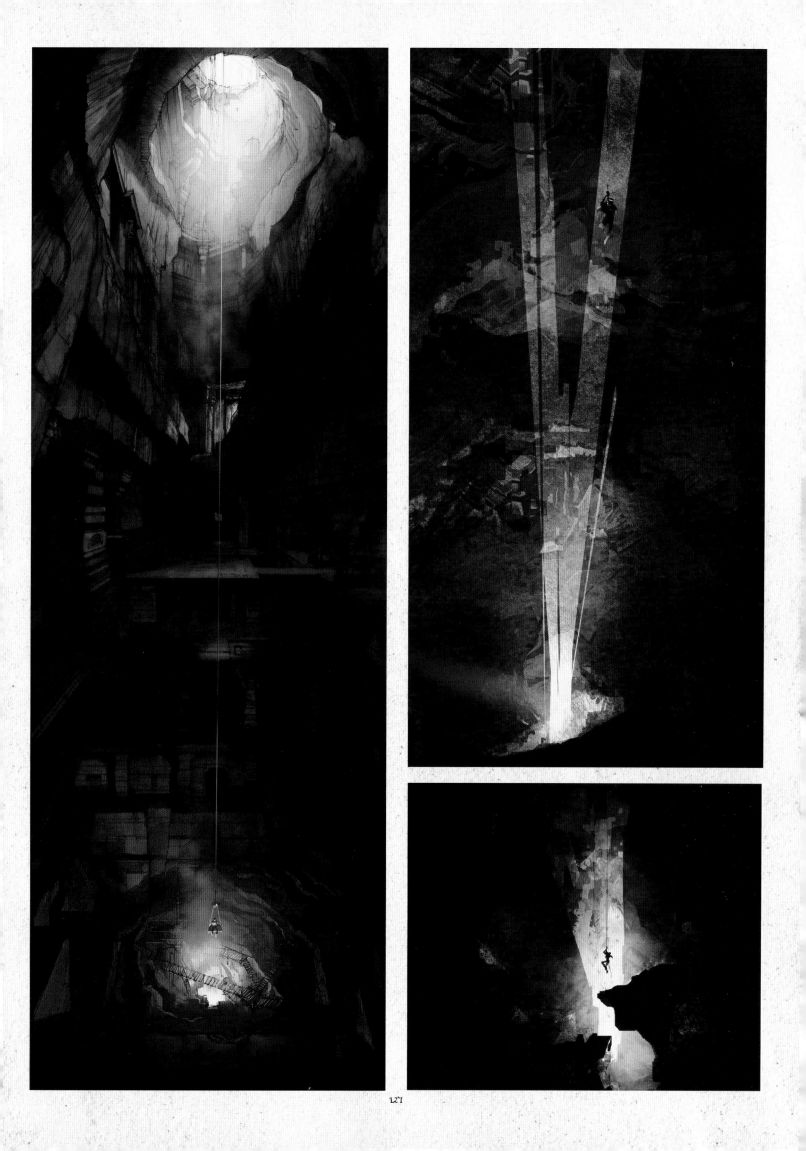

Cement Mixers, Cheese Graters, and a Touch of Genius

On a nondescript street in one of the grubbiest neighborhoods—appropriately known as the *Zone Industrielle*—in the otherwise enchanting Marrakesh stands an equally nondescript building. But in the months leading up to the filming of *Prince of Persia: The Sands of Time*, and during the duration of its Morocco shoot, this building was a dream factory, housing a small army of cutters, costumers, cobblers, seamstresses, milliners, dyers, armorers, and artisans, all working under the brilliant hegemony of costume designer Penny Rose.

"There's no one in her field like Penny," says Jerry Bruckheimer, who previously enlisted her prodigious skills for the entire Pirates of the Caribbean trilogy (it was Penny Rose who, with the collaboration of Bruckheimer, director Gore Verbinski and, of course, Johnny Depp, created the now-immortal look of Captain Jack Sparrow) as well as *King Arthur*. "Her attention to detail almost defies description," Bruckheimer continues, "and her ability to find the exact right costumes to define characters, and allow the actors to get comfortable in their clothing, is fantastic. Penny can organize anything, anywhere in the world. She's a tough taskmaster, but we love her artistry."

Actors who work with Penny Rose find themselves becoming almost fanatically devoted to her boundless creativity.

"Penny is phenomenal," enthuses Jake Gyllenhaal, "not only as a costume designer, but also as a coach. She's just full of humor. The character and wardrobe came alive together. The first thing you learn with Penny is that you're not going to wear anything for frills. It's all going to be functional, something you could use in battle. Every armband, strap of leather, or chest plate that Dastan wears is there for a reason."

"Penny is fond of the Orientalist school of painting," notes Sir Ben Kingsley, "and has completely understood the perspective, the dynamic, colors, tones, and light, helping to re-create the look on film. I noticed some extras resting on set, and they looked exactly like Orientalist paintings, absolutely exquisite—like paintings in fabric."

"Orientalist paintings were part of the influence," acknowledges Rose, taking a break from her usual tornado of activity. "Most of those images were painted in Victorian times, so they're

ABOVE: Penny Rose attends to the headdress of a background player costumed as an African warrior in the sequence of King Sharaman's funeral procession; OPPOSITE: The Orientalist painting by nineteenth century Russian artist Vasily Vereshchagin colorfully titled Political Debate in an Opium Den *shows its subjects wearing robes even more ragged than the one worn in the film by Sheikh Amar (Alfred Molina).*

nineteenth-century impressions of scenes from hundreds of years previous to that. The scale of the Orientalist pictures was the most significant thing to us: the shapes of the garments, the flowing cloaks, the amount of people crushed into small spaces."

For *Prince of Persia: The Sands of Time*, Penny Rose had to create no fewer than 7,000 costumes, nearly all of them built from scratch, so she assembled what she calls her "family": associate costume designer John Norster, assistant costume designer Margie Fortune, costume supervisor Ken Crouch, and costume designer assistant Lucy Bowring. Rose also relied heavily upon the on-set costumers for the principal actors. That team was led by wardrobe master Mark Holmes and included Ciara McArdle, Adam Roach, Nancy Thompson, Maurizio Torti, and Philip "Goldie" Goldsworthy.

"Penny's wardrobe warehouse was almost overwhelming," notes executive producer Chad Oman. "Thousands of pieces of clothing, racks and racks from one wall to the other in a huge building. Huge wooden canisters filled with boots and other footwear, then walls and walls of headgear and helmets. Artisans hand-tooling leather in one area, dyeing clothes in another, cutting in another corner. It's pretty impressive, to say the least."

The task of dressing hundreds of background players on the big crowd-scene days fell to Kenny Crouch. "Every one of those extras has to have their own identity," insists Rose. "When an assistant director hauls five hundred people onto the set, you can't be certain that two people in an identical costume won't be standing next to each other. So we take enormous care to give everybody an individual fitting so that they are a character of their own."

The genius of Penny Rose recalls an aspect of the work of René Magritte. The Belgian surrealist painted a famously vivid still life of a smoker's pipe, with the words *"Ceci n'est pas une pipe"* ("This is not a pipe") directly underneath. Penny Rose might look at a Persian rug and say "This is not a carpet. This is a pair of boots. Or perhaps ten pairs of boots." She sees three separate Indian bedspreads and envisions a raggedy coat of faded opulence for a self-important desert-bandit king. In Rose's world, what you see is not necessarily what you get.

Rose's process began with copious amounts of research, from which she assembled "mood boards" filled with images derived from paintings, photos, and illustrations. "We like to decorate the room with the mood boards because it gives the flavor of what we want to do, and it's a helpful everyday reminder."

To set up the workshop in Marrakesh, Rose enlisted a quartet she describes as "my secret weapon, four divine Italians": workshop supervisor Stefano De Nardis, assistant supervisor Maurizio Torti, head cutter Massimiliana Tiberi, and dyeing department supervisor Pamela Paolini, all Romans with previous experience working in Morocco. "Pamela would take someone who had never done a specific type of dyeing, and by lunch they had it," recalls Rose. "And the quantities going through her dye shop were extraordinary. She had twenty-four people, and there would be up to fifteen racks every day that needed to be done and out by the evening, and Pamela just plowed through." With giant bathtubs and huge burners, Paolini and her workers did what Moroccans have been doing for thousands of years. "If you've seen the great dye pits in the Fez medina, then you know that dyeing is a specialty in Morocco," notes Rose.

Penny Rose also enlisted the skills of Moroccan artisans, many of them found in the Marrakesh medina and other souks. "Our shoemaker was extraordinary. I could bring him a rug I'd found that day, and by lunch they had made three pairs of boots out of it! And the leather maker made Jake's fighting costume, which is just a work of art." There was also a small room toward the back of the facility in which the Moroccan metalworkers created beautifully complex jewelry and other items to be either worn or incorporated into the costumes.

Another trick of Penny Rose's trade, unimaginable to those outside the craft, is the breakdown department, which was under the supervision of Gildardo Tobon. "Gil did the Pirates movies and knows how we like it," says Rose. "In general, very few people on the films I do go to set in a new costume. We always have to break it down first. I want costumes to look real, even in a fantasy film like *Prince of Persia: The Sands of Time*. Gil brought a crew of his own with him, and we set them up in a big section of the warehouse. They have their tools of the trade, including a cement mixer. Once the leather goods are newly made, we put them in the cement mixer for a couple of hours with a few stones, and they come out looking well used. They also use cheese graters to distress costumes, believe it or not."

To obtain the materials for so many thousands of costumes, Rose scoured the four corners of the globe. "We have a wonderful buyer, Roz Ward, who has worked with us over many years and knows our taste. That's the key, because you can't say specifically, 'Get me fifty meters of this or ten yards of that.' You just need someone who has the right eye who's a party to the research when it's being done. We sent Roz first to Chiang

Mai, Thailand, which not only has a wonderful fabric-textile source but also has lots of villages where they are physically being made. Roz then went to India to buy in big quantities. We had someone else go to Turkey. We get a lot of items from Turkey, because we like their tent decorations and wall hangings. All sorts of Turkish fabrics and textiles can be chopped up and ingrained into the costumes. We bought many things from Afghanistan, through a lady in Los Angeles, and then we went to Paris and Rome.

"We buy a lot at the flea market in Paris," continues Rose. "It's our main source of trim. We have a fantastic contact there who has very big quantities, because when you're making six or twelve coats or tunics, you might need two hundred meters of braid." Also in the Parisian flea markets, Rose's buyers obtained a bizarre array of items that were ingeniously recycled into on-screen works of art. "We'll buy broken chandeliers, door hinges, and handles, because we can then mold them for all kinds of things."

Other countries contributing their fabrics to Rose's costume department were China, Malaysia, Great Britain and, of course, Morocco.

With fabric and color, Penny Rose created two completely different identities for the Persians and the fictitious Alamutians. "Persia was taking advantage of the Silk Road, even in the sixth century, when our film is set, and they knew the fruit and vegetable sources that would give them the best colors. So the Persian costumes are saturated with jewel-like color, some of them quite ornate. As a contrast, because Alamut is a mystical and gentle society, we made all of their costumes in a cream color, very soothing to the eye."

Dastaŋ

"As anyone can see, Jake Gyllenhaal has a superb body," notes Penny Rose. "And we felt that it was relevant to show elements of it without a kind of full-on torso. So we start the movie in his battle armor, which was painstakingly made in real leather—with all the ingredients and accessories— by a wonderful Moroccan craftsman. It is a big wink at the video game, be- cause we felt there had to be an identity from the first frame, so audiences will recognize aspects of the look from the games. For riding and stunts, we had a plastic replica, much lighter, but you can barely tell the difference.

"For Jake's second costume, the inspi- ration for his coat came from an old piece of textile we picked up in an antique fair," Rose continues. "I particularly liked the work on it, thought it had a very good identity of its own. So we remade it by hand and turned it into a coat, bound by leather. Jake loves what we call the 'spiral coat' because it's really light, he can really move in it. He's got a white linen shirt with hand- stitching down the front and on the cuffs, plus a sash and a belt, and a nice necklace. Jake wears boots and knee protectors with this costume.

"But I think Jake's favorite costume is when he's dis- guised as an Indian palanquin-bearer for a very large Mu- ghal in King Sharaman's funeral procession. It's metallic- embroidered red silk from India, and I must say that Jake cuts rather a dash in it, especially with the matching headdress."

ABOVE: Racks of costumes in the huge wardrobe department warehouse in Marrakesh's Zone Industrielle; RIGHT: Illustration by Darrell Warner of a Penny Rose design for one of Dastan's costumes.

Tamina

We first see Tamina in the film in her chambers in Ala-mut, and I thought it would be a good moment to give an aesthetically beautiful flavor to what she wears," explains Rose. "But I also wanted to show off Gemma's figure. She's got great legs and a tiny waist, and I just thought we should do something wafty but corseted. So we made her a beautiful, simple, light dress, introducing a little bit of gold to it. The dress also has a beautifully embroidered cape and hood. It looks very glamorous, and I think it also makes her slightly untouchable, so that when the Persians first see her it makes them stand back a bit. We needed Tamina to be in her Sunday best, but also layer the costume so that when she escapes with Dastan from Alamut, she could lose some of it, because it was too grand for the rough-and-tumble action scenes.

"So Tamina ends up with just a pair of trousers and a long tunic," adds Rose. "Our research revealed that the ladies of the time had huge pantaloons underneath their tunics, but for riding purposes I gave Gemma a slimmer type of trouser, which also shows off Tamina's tomboy side.

"For the scene in which Tamina is captured by Sheikh Amar, we had great fun creating a sort of Bedouin serving-wench look for Gemma: lots of flesh, very tatty, shredded, and filthy. And then we give her a dazzling Indian outfit when she's posing—along with Dastan—as a Mughal-bearing servant. We've kept all of Tamina's colors very beige and pale, and light, because we knew that she was going to be working in 120-degree Moroccan heat."

Nizam

Sir Ben and I had a chat about Nizam in preproduction," recalls Penny Rose, "and decided that his character would be a dandy. And to that end, Sir Ben has more changes of costume than anyone, about a dozen in all. We decided that Nizam loves tassels, that he would be heavily brocaded. We decided immediately that Nizam would have no head gear. . . . One of Sir Ben's strengths is his wonderful head, and we didn't want to cover it, although we did develop some headdresses for the flashback sequences."

Sheikh Amar

"We decided immediately that Sheikh Amar never changes his clothing," says Penny Rose. "He should have one iconic look, and that would be it. He's a vagabond, kind of a street person of the desert, so I needed to emphasize the raggedness. We created a light tunic and trousers, but the coat was a challenge. We finally made it from three or four vintage Indian bedspreads layered to create a robe. Then we took a cheese grater to it until we got this fantastic ragged look, revealing layers of different fabrics, colors, and designs. The sheikh also has a headdress, and his boots are made from an old carpet."

"The coat looks like it's made up of a thousand pieces of material," says Alfred Molina. "It's a beautiful piece of work, and when it was nice, it looked gorgeous. We thought that maybe the sheikh stole the coat from some prince. . . . But it's been a while since that's happened, and he's been living in it, sleeping in it, fighting in it. So Penny took a cheese grater to it in the most vicious way, and what you see [appears to be] the result of years and years of wear and tear."

Seso

Explains Rose, "We needed Seso's African background to be prominent, and we really felt that it was essential to keep his princely flavor despite the fact that the sheikh and most of his men are displaced persons who have fallen from glory. Seso is draped in a rather complicated ocher wrap with a leopard-skin cape, and Steve Toussaint looks fantastic in it."

garsiv and tus

Garsiv, as a warrior, will not be parted from his armor, and neither would Toby Kebbell," laughs Rose. "He has five different costumes, but will only wear his armor on top. I didn't fight him, because it helped Toby with the character—no problem for us. He looked great in it. But it was fascinating how determined he was from day one to never take it off. And to Toby's eternal credit, he didn't complain even when it was one hundred and twenty degrees. And as Garsiv, he really does look like a warrior. You wouldn't want to meet him on a dark night."

Responds Kebbell, "It's an honor to wear Penny's costumes. I can't describe it any other way. The armor alone is phenomenal, and when you wear it you instantly feel like the character. These costumes are so beautifully designed, and it's baffling to see the kind of effort that goes into helping you become someone else."

"As for Richard Coyle's Prince Tus," says Rose, "I felt that he wasn't the warrior who actually goes into battle—he's the one giving the orders. And I felt that we needed to know immediately that he was the king in waiting. So he's quite smart, lavishly dressed with expensive silk material and all the trimmings."

King Sharaman

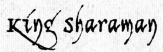

Penny Rose's account of creating the wardrobe for Ronald Pickup as King Sharaman is a fascinating example of her creative process. "I wanted Ronnie Pickup's costume as King Sharaman to have a huge impact," notes Rose. "A sample was sent to me from an upholstery shop in Rome of a burgundy-colored silk with a huge gold embroidered pattern on it, and I just had to have it. But we discovered that the pattern might look more like curtains when actually worn by an actor. So we ordered some of the burgundy silk plain, cut the gold pieces off the other one and planted them where they should be, down the front and on the cuffs. And then, to salvage my conscience over the cost of the fabric, I found in a box of mine three identical saris that I'd been carrying around since the first Pirates of the Caribbean, and they became his robe, so I felt that I had equaled out the expense! It's a beautiful gown, and really suits him.

"Then we had to create the poisoned cloak that kills King Sharaman," Rose continues. "I discovered a pleated cape in a book about ancient Persian dress, which I thought looked pretty spectacular. Then one morning, at six o'clock on Portobello Road, we saw a roll of fabric that had metal shopped through it, pliable and stiff at the same time. So we sent it to the pleaters, and it came out fantastically well."

THE ARMORY

Whether working from his specially tricked-out truck in the burning heat of Morocco or from a chilly and drafty corrugated-metal workshop at Pinewood Studios, Richard Hooper was the go-to guy for all things deliciously deadly on *Prince of Persia: The Sands of Time*. As a motion-picture armorer, Hooper can provide the appropriate weapons for every kind of project, from the ultra contemporary (*Batman Begins, Casino Royale*) to the futuristic (*Children of Men, Wanted*) to the historic (*Alexander*), with nary a hitch.

"On *Prince of Persia*," Hooper informs, "everything was created from scratch, designed or concept-approved by the art department, the producer, the director, or the actor, and then executed.

"The main design influence of the Persian weaponry came from research of sixth-century design, and also was influenced by the Prince of Persia video game," Hooper continues. "I tried to find a balance between historic authenticity and fantasy, because Jerry Bruckheimer and Mike Newell wanted us to travel that fine line down the middle. They're both very precise about what they want and what they think audiences will like. We researched the collections in museums in Iran, Turkey, Iraq, Egypt, the British Museum in London, the Smithsonian. And we found various books containing the armor and weapons of Persia at that time. We picked and chose various styles and elements, then created our own designs of the swords, daggers, and shields."

Hooper and his department created close to 3,500 individual items, including swords, shields, spears, axes, arrows, bows, quivers, scabbards, bow cases, daggers, and Hassanin weapons. The weaponry was fabricated from iron, wood, and rubber, or whatever was required for an individual scene. And like other creative department heads on the film, Hooper would rely on the fine artisanship found in Morocco. "Morocco is a great place to do a film of this type, because you can utilize the great skills of the country's artisans," notes Hooper. "From leather workers to metal engravers and cloth makers, there are many skills that people have completely forgotten in developed countries like England and America. [Moroccans] are also absolutely brilliant in transcribing Middle Eastern styles from a book or a drawing into reality, because they're living their heritage and history."

In his Marrakesh workshop, Hooper had fifteen crew members from the U.K. and twenty-five Moroccans. "For close-ups, the weapons would be made from stainless steel or cast metals, with silver or gold plating. We use durable rubber versions for large-scale battle scenes."

Each character has his or her own distinctive weapons; for example, Dastan's twin swords with their eagle- and lion-shaped hilts (a very deliberate nod to the video game), Tamina's ornate dagger, and Seso's African throwing knives, with their ivory hilts sculpted to resemble the face of a noble warrior. Then, of course, there are the Hassansins, each of whom is actually defined by his weapon: a giant scimitar; a double halberd; Greek fire grenades; projectile darts; menacing arm guards that shoot out a mean blade and three-prong fork; and whips tipped with vicious blades. Thankfully, Richard Hooper was not responsible for lead Hassansin Zolm's primary weapon—deadly vipers.

LEFT to RIGHT: Armorer Richard Hooper demonstrates some of his work to Jon Rogers of Walt Disney Studios Motion Picture's franchise development division; illustrations of Tamina's ornate dagger, Dastan's "hero" sword with its eagle-shaped hilt, Ghazab's double halberd, and Hassad's blade-tipped whip. The final version of the halberd is depicted above, with Domonkos Pardanyi as Ghazab and Claudio Pacifico as Setam.

A Whirlwind of Action

W hat a bizarre sight it must have been for the residents of the leafy middle-class neighborhood surrounding the Kawkab Training Pitch in the central part of the Nouvelle Ville (New City) of Marrakesh, to see what was happening on their local football field. Instead of players kicking the soccer ball around, there were almost 100 very fit gentlemen (and some ladies as well), most of them in tracksuits or even less, pummeling each other with a fantastic array of prop swords, halberds, daggers, whips, spears, and other implements of mass havoc. What the Moroccans were witnessing was stunt coordinator George Aguilar and his team of fearless adventurers, training and rehearsing for the stupendous action scenes in *Prince of Persia: The Sands of Time*.

From fantastic parkour displays of gravity- and death-defying leaps and acrobatics to outrageous ostrich races to medieval Near Eastern battles on a grand scale, the film gave its stunt coordinators an epic canvas on which to paint great swirls of action. The daring team was comprised of first-unit stunt coordinator Aguilar, second-unit stunt coordinator Greg Powell, Morocco co-stunt coordinator Stephen Pope, co-fight coordinators Thomas Dupont and Ben Cooke, and parkour adviser David Belle (*see* separate story) with their huge cast of stunt players, not to mention the stars of the film. Jerry Bruckheimer's productions are known for some of the most elaborate and imaginative action set pieces in screen history, and *Prince of Persia: The Sands of Time* is no exception. The Persian attack on Alamut, and Dastan's commando raid that precedes it; Dastan and Tamina's escape from Alamut; the frenetically funny ostrich race; Dastan eluding Persian soldiers in the Avrat Bazaar; the battle with the Hassansins both in the desert oasis and the Hidden Valley; Dastan and Tamina eluding dangers in the substructure beneath Alamut; and Dastan and Nizam's suspenseful face-off at the Sandglass of the Gods . . . these scenes would all test the mettle of the stars, the stunt teams in both units, and the filmmakers.

For the actors, preparation began several weeks before the cameras began to turn, with rigorous training programs designed to whip them into shape and get them on horseback. Jake Gyllenhaal was already in prime physical condition as an avid runner, bicyclist, and all-around athlete, but underwent a punishing training regimen before and during filming.

LEFT: Dastan (Jake Gyllenhaal) fights off Nizam's (Ben Kingsley) men on the Alamut Palace stairs; ABOVE: Dastan catches up with Tamina (Gemma Arterton) in the desert.

"There's no reason to do a movie like this," says Gyllenhaal, "if you can't do the stunts. It was all about functional fitness, being able to do everything that was asked of me. So I got into the best shape I could, with a lot of running, parkour training, weight lifting, and

horseback riding." Indeed, one of the aspects of portraying Dastan that appealed to Gyllenhaal was the character's great physicality: "The movies I've always loved are the ones in which the characters have the capability to do almost anything, but still be a human being and not a superhero. When Dastan jumps or leaps, it's all within the realm of possibility. It just goes beyond that level of what you're used to seeing. And in fact, when we do stunts on set, they're the real thing. We often do them without wires, and I think an audience will really pick up on that, because we're so used to seeing movies in which everything is done with computers."

Along with the other cast members, Gyllenhaal also did extensive training with horses under the tutelage of Ricardo Cruz Moral, one of Spain's top equestrians, at Moral's ranch outside of Madrid. For Gemma Arterton, it was a revelation: "I'd never ridden a horse in my life, so I was sent away with the others on a kind of horse-riding boot camp before we started the film. It was brilliant, and now horseback riding is one of my hobbies. One of the stunts in the film that I do myself is when I'm swept onto a horse as it's coming towards me, and I was really proud of that.

"We have an amazing stunt crew on this film," Arterton continues, "and we had quite an extensive training period in preproduction at Ealing Studios outside of London. Tamina is a high priestess and quite anti-war, so we decided that when she fights it's kind of untrained and quite wild. I hit people over the head a lot. . . . I think that's Tamina's signature move."

Sir Ben Kingsley enjoyed the fact that, while training and filming the action sequences, "I'm in my body and not in my head, and that's a great place to be." As for Alfred Molina, portraying Sheikh Amar, a character who avoids physical danger at all costs, "While the others were spending hours learning how to kill each other, I was basically out sightseeing and enjoying Moroccan pizzas," he laughs. For Steve Toussaint, portraying the expert knife-thrower Seso, "the training never really stopped. From the beginning in Morocco to the end in England, there was continuous combat and knife training."

"This is the hardest work I've ever done," agrees Toby Kebbell. "And rightly so. We're making an action film that has to look absolutely genuine. There was no going out to dinner and quaffing drinks till the late hours. It was, you wake up, go to work, get your makeup and costume on, and get your head focused. You needed that kind of dedication. Jake was the master of it, I have to say. He's supposed to be the chap who can run up walls and back flip over a canyon, and Jake never stopped training, day in and day out."

Kebbell now admits that when he was first interviewed by Mike Newell and asked if he could ride a horse, he flat-out fibbed. "I had a basic idea of what they *looked* like, but none at all about *riding* them," he now says with a laugh. He certainly did after weeks of training under Cruz Moral and his Spanish crew. "It was beautiful to be at the ranch with Ricardo and his guys," says Kebbell. "We really all took it incredibly seriously. You know, you're working with amazing stunt people like George Aguilar, Ben Cooke, and Tom Dupont, who are teaching you these incredible skills with weaponry. The shoot was incredibly physical, so it was necessary to do all of that incredibly hard training."

"When we started rehearsing at the football pitch, it was as if someone pulled the switch and turned up the heat," recalls Dupont. "It was like a hair dryer with zero humidity. We went through a lot of water and took plenty of breaks, but we got through it because we had a common goal—to make a great movie."

Stunt coordinator George Aguilar, who had worked with director Mike Newell on *Donnie Brasco*, was excited by the myriad challenges of the film. "The sword fights, the parkour, the ostrich race, the supernatural elements, it was all so challenging," says Aguilar. "Jerry Bruckheimer and Mike Newell wanted an epic feel to the stunts but with a new twist, incorporating parkour into epic battles and fights." Aguilar assembled a team of seventy international stunt players—hailing from the United States, Great Britain, Spain, Slovakia, France, and Italy—as well as an additional fifty Moroccans while filming in that country. "We had quite a United Nations of stunt people," notes Aguilar. Morocco has a great tradition of daredevil Berber horsemen (nearly all tourists have at one point or another experienced a dazzling display of their equestrian skills in a heart-pounding "fantasia"), and several extraordinary riders amply demonstrated their skills during production there.

Thomas Dupont, whose work on the Pirates of the Caribbean films took great advantage of his expert sword-fighting skills, served on *Prince of Persia: The Sands of Time* as co-fight coordinator, with Ben Cooke. Dupont also portrayed the lethal Hassad, a Hassansin who fights with two blade-tipped whips. Explaining the challenges of shooting a big action scene at an elevation of 8,200 feet, (the Hassansin attack on Dastan and company in the Hidden Valley), Dupont notes, "As far as the altitude was concerned, the hardest part was the sustained fighting. We had to do a lot of things at once for up to a minute at a time. Now, that may not seem like a long time, but if you're performing at full energy, with strikes, running, and jumping, that tends to wind you. And if you're already up eight thousand feet and the oxygen is scarce, it really takes its toll."

Working right alongside George Aguilar and Alexander Witt, the film's second-unit director, was second-unit stunt coordinator Greg Powell, who began his career as a stuntman in his native Britain at the age of fourteen. Alex Witt and Greg Powell's great experience and expertise made a huge contribution to the film's action sequences. "This movie has been an adventure," Powell noted toward the last days of filming at Pinewood Studios. "We've taken nearly every stage at the studio, plus half of the Moroccan desert. It's been great fun. Jake is capable of doing it all himself, and we only use his stunt doubles when it's absolutely impossible for safety reasons."

"We wanted to establish that Dastan's got quite a flashy style, but also that he's dangerous, in command, and a warrior," adds Ben Cooke. "Jake has to fight convincingly with two swords and a dagger, in addition to the parkour and free-running elements, and that's a lot to learn. But Jake's done it. . . . He's rocked the party. When he gets in there, he knocks it out. We'll have him fighting, jumping, falling, sometimes up on rigs that are forty or fifty feet up in the air. Jake's all for it."

"I learned at the foot of people who have designed some of the most insane movie fights you've ever seen," enthuses Gyllenhaal. "We did a ton of fight rehearsals. I remember the first one that we did, just learning how to do simple moves, starting with a strike and parry, and slowly moving on to much more difficult choreography. It's sort of funny, because by the time we were on day ninety-eight, I walked onto set, and Ben Cooke says, 'Okay, mates, you're gonna parry him off, turn around, then he's gonna come around here and swipe under your head,' and I was like, 'Okay, no problem.' It's amazing how you start to take it all for granted once you've gotten used to the process."

DAVID BELLE:
A PASSION FOR PARKOUR

A wiry, compact man in his mid-thirties with short hair and a slim but powerful frame could often be found inspecting the Avrat rooftops set on D Stage at Pinewood Studios. Nothing less than the creator of a contemporary physical art form with deep roots in ancient disciplines, this man was thrilled to have been summoned by Jerry Bruckheimer to devote his talents and energies to *Prince of Persia: The Sands of Time*. He's David Belle, a young legend, and the originator of parkour.

"We wanted the best of the best, and that's David Belle," says Jerry Bruckheimer. "We decided to go right to the source."

"In the video game, the prince can run up walls and has other skills based on parkour," explains director Mike Newell. "Parkour started in the suburbs of Paris, where the kids were so bored that they started to use what was available to them as some kind of test. I watched documentaries about them and saw that they really do walk up walls and leap from rooftop to rooftop. They are extraordinary athletes. So we brought some of the great world experts of parkour to teach us what to do and how to make it look good."

"It's like a child's dream come true," mused Belle, observing the expertly detailed contours of the huge set, its earthen buildings and ancient architecture a close match for actual locations in Morocco. "This is the kind of film that makes me wish I was in the movie industry. When you watch this type of movie, it's so magnificent that you want to be a part of the scene. And all of a sudden I find that I'm here on this set."

Belle was originally approached at the start of filming to join the production, but at that point he was otherwise occupied. "I was already working on my own movie, *District 13—Ultimatum*, so I couldn't accept the proposal. I was so upset that I couldn't participate and thought that I would regret it later, so when I got another call some months later, I was so happy that I could finally be available."

Belle wasn't the only one. "Fortunately for Dastan, he's well versed in parkour," notes Jerry Bruckheimer. "And so, when he's being pursued, he can escape by running up walls, climbing, and jumping over objects, and we hired David Belle, the best in the world, to consult and help create action sequences and train the actors. Bruckheimer continues, "The parkour element comes from the game itself. It's really an art form. It's so exciting to watch people literally bouncing off of walls, all done without wires, doing it through their own physical force."

In French, parkour is also known as "*l'art du déplacement*," or the art of movement. And indeed, to its practitioners and those who observe the astounding feats of *traceurs*—practitioners of parkour—it is nothing less than wondrous. The action of *Prince of Persia: The Sands of Time* incorporates both parkour and its offshoot, free running.

David Belle's own description of parkour is, as one would imagine coming from the man responsible for its present form, perfectly concise and lucid. "To make it simple, parkour is a training method that allows a person to develop their physique so that they can overcome obstacles. The more you train, the faster and more efficient you become. When training, you can create a wide range of movements. These movements help you to get through difficult passageways, between buildings, and over rooftops. It's a different way to learn to move your body."

Belle has been developing parkour for more than twenty years, but acknowledges that many of the principles existed before him and were part of his own family's tradition. "It wasn't me who created parkour. My contribution to parkour is bringing my father's story to life. He was a legendary firefighter and believed that keeping physically fit was necessary to decrease risk and avoid potentially disastrous mistakes. My father passed his knowledge of parkour on to me.

"The difference between real parkour and stunts is that in the film you have to take into consideration the beauty and the thrill of the scene, even if sometimes it isn't the most logical solution. I felt as if the Avrat Bazaar set was created especially for parkour. As Dastan is walking in the bazaar, he is already thinking about everything around him, such as the placement of the windows in the houses and the beams in the ceilings. Being a choreographer, I am able to be on the outside and analyze the situation, like Dastan, where normally I am in the heart of it. I can think of different movements that would work and at the same time make parkour mesh well with the plot. I try to offer the director as many choices as possible without having to move around objects and waste precious time. If one thing doesn't work, then we find something else right away. I always think a bit in advance of what might not work, and, in general, each suggestion I made was logical and in keeping with the plotline."

Belle was impressed by Jake Gyllenhaal's parkour abilities and the enthusiasm with which the actor quite literally threw himself into the action. "Jake certainly had me convinced," he says. "I've seen his work, his movements in various scenes, and I have no doubt." Adds stunt coordinator George Aguilar, "Jake does everything, and more often than not without a wire. What we think he can get away with, and what he thinks he can get away with, Jake tries. He's done some really big jumps, both distance- and height-wise. It's only when there's something really dangerous that we ask Jake's parkour doubles, Mark Fichera and Bobby Panton, to temporarily fill in for him."

David Belle's passion for parkour began in childhood and has never flagged. "When I was fourteen, I liked combining all of the movements, such as climbing trees or jumping walls, and making them something specific and useful in the real world. I realized that there was a difference between parkour and other sports, where you need accessories. With parkour, you can adapt to all situations, no matter the day, the time, the weather. When you are able to jump, climb, hang in the air, it means that you are in good physical condition. It's like when you can pick up a book and read without making mistakes, you know your brain is in good health. It's really a complete sport that makes you at ease with all other sports."

In David Belle's world of parkour, you can't run and jump before you learn how to crawl. But once you *can* run and jump, there are no limits.

OPPOSITE ABOVE: David Belle perched high atop the Avrat rooftops set at Pinewood Studios;
BELOW: An incredible parkour feat accomplished by stuntman and traceur Mark Fichera.

Rewinds, Extensions, and other Magic

With precedents like *Armageddon*, *Pearl Harbor*, or any of the three Pirates of the Caribbean films—all of which were nominated for Academy Awards for visual effects, with *Pirates of the Caribbean: Dead Man's Chest* taking the little golden guy home—one thing that viewers have come to expect from Jerry Bruckheimer films is movie wizardry that represents a quantum leap. "Just when you think that you've seen just about everything," says the producer, "we stand visual effects on their ear and do things that haven't been seen before. Hopefully, what you'll see on screen in *Prince of Persia: The Sands of Time* will be something fresh, interesting, and innovative."

A casual observer might have thought that the well-tanned, tallish chap in the turban, often striding purposefully around on the set in Morocco, was one of the local crew members. Upon closer investigation, however, that observer would have discovered that it was actually British visual-effects supervisor Tom Wood, who, like so many others in the company, was sensible enough to adorn himself in native headdress for protection against the merciless North African midsummer sun.

A good thing, too, because Wood had too much on his plate to allow himself to succumb to heatstroke. *Prince of Persia: The Sands of Time* is a film in which state-of-the-art visual effects play an absolutely crucial role. What good is a movie about a dagger that rewinds time without the movie magic that makes that happen on-screen? How can a filmmaker depict epic cities

and landscapes that stem from real sets and natural settings? Ultimately, Tom Wood and his extensive team of producers, managers, coordinators, data wranglers, and technicians would be called upon to create some 1,200 visual-effects shots for the film. Some were long and involved—such as the time rewinds and the massive climactic sequence beneath Alamut—and some were minor little fixes at the edge of a frame.

For his work, Wood would enlist all of the modern technologies and techniques at his command. Considering the subtitle of the movie, the most important effects for Wood were the four time rewinds, caused when the jewel on the hilt of the dagger is pushed, releasing the Sands of Time. "We decided immediately that we couldn't just run the film backwards," explains Wood. "We didn't want it to look like a VCR rewind. We had to develop an original and visually interesting approach. What we aimed for was a kind of slit-scan effect where everything would be warped by time and space.

"What we've done for the time rewind was designed by Double Negative, the visual-effects house we've hired," Wood continues. "They call it 'event capture,' and we're trying to create a new look and a very new approach. We've pre-visualized this sequence thoroughly over the last four months, with 'animatics' resembling animated storyboards. We then came onto the main unit set and shot the forward-running action, followed by four days of effects coverage, putting cameras in the positions that we wanted to capture a shot from.

OPPOSITE BELOW: *The Sands of Time swirl around and within Dastan after he's pressed the jewel of the Dagger, thus reversing time itself;* ABOVE: *Tus (Richard Coyle) gazes down at the city of Alamut—originally a blue screen at Pinewood Studios and later a detailed panorama provided by CG artists;* RIGHT *and* BELOW: *Images depicting the development of the setting for King Sharaman's funeral procession, beginning with the original Moroccan location and ending with the final CG-rendered environment and leopard statues.*

ABOVE and RIGHT: The magic of CG is evident in these before and after images that demonstrate the transformation of the Moroccan desert into the magical landscape of Alamut, enhanced with greenery, mountains, and cloud-dappled skies; OPPOSITE BELOW: One of lead Hassansin Zolm's deadly vipers, entirely created by CG artists.

"We have nine Arriflex 435 cameras shooting with identical lenses, up to forty-eight frames a second at a forty-five-degree shutter angle, which has caused a lot of challenges with relighting the set," continues Wood. "That's to get as sharp an image as possible. We have a number of people from Double Negative who have laid out the cameras each time, surveyed into position. They have to be very precise. We can't go any wider than a seventeen-degree separation between any two cameras to stop a collusion where, say, a hand gets in front of a face and we don't have information for that face. It takes about two hours to set up each array of cameras.

"So we've had to have our principal actors doing twenty minutes of acting, and then they have to go away for two hours, come back for another twenty minutes, and remember where they were and the action from their main-unit forward-running shot," adds Wood. "For the first time rewind sequence, for example, Tamina is trying to get the Dagger of Time away from Dastan. He doesn't know there's anything magical about it, but finds out when he accidentally presses the jeweled button and time rewinds for about thirty seconds. He comes out of that stunned, but realizes that the Dagger is immensely special and precious.

"When time runs backwards, we didn't want to just have the same actions in reverse. We wanted the effect to have a very treated visual-effects look, as photographic as we can make it. We established what the overall blocking of the action was, which was predetermined. We came in with the main unit and shot the forwards action, and in that process, Mike Newell and director of photography John Seale changed it slightly, and the actors obviously have their input into these shots and the action, so the characterization is much fuller than the pre-visualization. At the same time, we've been taking notes throughout so we can hit those beats as well as repeat that action. Then Jake and Gemma have to come back and go through their moves with us, and that's a problem, trying to keep it fresh for each time that we see it."

The arduous filming of the time rewind sequences obviously challenged the actors' abilities of recall and concentration. "I'd never done visual-effects sequences before, and it's a really, really long process," admits Gemma Arterton. "But when you see it, it looks magical, adding a whole other dimension to the film."

Having previously worked in Morocco on Ridley Scott's *Kingdom of Heaven*, for which he helped to create a virtual ancient Jerusalem, Tom Wood was pleased to return to North Africa to extend Wolf Kroeger's already stupendous environments. "The sets have been fantastic, so for the Morocco shoot we had very clear ideas of how we could extend the cities," says Wood. "We're creating three virtual cities, one Persian, one Alamutian, and another kind of Valley-of-the-Kings style one where King Sharaman is buried. We're seeing them from the ground, from the air, traveling through them—just an enormous amount of work. But, at the same time, it's a joy to work on because within this film there's a degree of Orientalist stylization so that we can push the boundaries. These are certainly environments based more in fantasy than historical realism." To create the mystical city of Alamut, Wood engaged in what he calls "a huge collaboration between the art department and the VFX department. We had computer models built of the city within the art department while we were in Morocco, from the conceptual paintings. Those models were then taken to The Moving Picture Company, which further developed them. They also sent one of their texture photographers to India for about three weeks, who came back with 15,000 stills of Jodhpur, Jaipur, and Jaisalmer in Rajasthan. They then built the huge fantasy city of Alamut using Indian elements, but also a lot of imagination."

Other issues that cropped up in creating the final version of Alamut were that the set was built on only one level although the conceptual art indicated a city mounted on rising levels; and it was also supposed to be green and lush as a contrast to the monochromatic desert city of Nasaf. Problem was, the huge practical Alamut set was constructed in the brown, dusty village of Tamesloht. "Alamut is a conical-shaped city topped with a very tall tower," notes Wood, "and wherever you are in the city you should be able to see the rest of it rising above you. So we've

had to put in backgrounds of hills and buildings surrounded by trees, sometimes with heavy rain clouds in the background. It never actually rained on that location, but we're pushing towards a sort of lush, humid look, so we created the weather digitally."

One can only wonder what the inhabitants of the ancient UNESCO World Heritage Site, the Kasbah of Ait Ben Haddou, will think when they see their earthen buildings magically converted into the royal Persian city of Nasaf. "Wolf Kroeger's set is really extensive, but still didn't cover what we want to represent in this city," noted Wood during filming at the foot of the kasbah. "We'll be augmenting the real sets, and extending beyond the edge of the physical set. Ait Ben Haddou sits on a desert plain and takes on the monochromatic colors of its environment, but we're going to digitally paint it with lots of passionate colors, including turquoise, orange, and purple, in what will look like a whitewash finish, and add a very grand palace at the top."

For *Prince of Persia: The Sands of Time*, Tom Wood en-listed some of the world's top visual-effects houses to work with him in creating specific sequences: the aforementioned Double Negative, for the time rewinds and Sandglass of the Gods; Framestore, for the pit vipers and the sand draining from the massive underground chamber in the climax of the film; Cinesite, for the Nasaf and Avrat city extensions; and The Moving Picture Company, for the Alamut extensions.

Meanwhile, another Wood—Trevor Wood (no relation to Tom), a veteran of British cinema who won an Academy Award for his work on *The Golden Compass*—was handling the special physical effects for the film with his talented team. Nearly fifty souls worked to create massive explosions, barriers of fire, burning oil, underground earthquakes, and all manner of mayhem on an epic scale. "We interact with nearly all other departments," explains Trevor Wood, "set dressing, props, and, obviously, the visual-effects department with Tom Wood. Tom and I work closely together just sorting out the crossover points between what will be a visual effect and what will be a practical effect. Hopefully, our mechanical effects will make the visual effects look even better."

A perfect example of this symbiotic relationship between visual and physical effects occurred in the oasis scene, in which Dastan and the others fight off pit vipers launched by the Hassansins. On the amazingly authentic oasis set at Pinewood Studios, Trevor Wood and his crew built a rig that lifted the sand as if snakes were slithering through it and another rig that fired green snake-like "sausages" out of the ground. These stand-ins would later be replaced by terrifyingly realistic computer-generated vipers.

"It's a very big undertaking," concludes Trevor Wood, "and whilst visual effects do take some of the work away from us, in the grander scheme of things they also produce a lot of work for us that the audience doesn't even see."

Mad Dogs, Englishmen, and a Few Thousand Others

Everybody said to us, 'Morocco's a great place,'" recalls Mike Newell. "'Just don't go there in July and August.' So of course, we shot all the way through July and August, because we couldn't not. We were hemmed in by dates. And, so you know, once in a while, people fell over. Not very much, actually, but you had to watch out for it."

"I couldn't understand why my hotel was empty when I got to Morocco," confesses Alfred Molina, who played Sheikh Amar. "I kept thinking, isn't everybody in Europe on holiday in August? And the local people were looking at me as if to say, *What are you* doing *here?* And then I quickly discovered that you don't go to Morocco then, 'cause it's too bloody hot! Nobody works in Morocco in August. So, yeah, mad dogs and Englishmen, I guess . . ."

"Mad dogs and Englishmen go out in the midday sun," twitters the 1930s Noel Coward ditty. While filming in Morocco from July through September 2008, it wasn't only mad dogs and Englishmen (although both were often seen in large numbers) but also Americans, Australians, Italians, Icelanders, Spaniards, Frenchmen, Chileans, Slovakians, Lithuanians—the whole League of Nations also known as the cast and crew of *Prince of Persia: The Sands of Time.* Some 550 members of the international community descended upon the North African kingdom, joined by more than 800 Moroccans proudly adding another notch to their country's ever-lengthening cinematic belt.

"It makes perfect sense to film a movie about the ancient world in Morocco," says producer Jerry Bruckheimer, "because the ancient and the modern coexist side by side. Even with chic restaurants, elegant clubs, and boutique hotels springing up all over Marrakesh, artisans in the medina are still hand-tooling their products just as they have for thousands of years. And outside of the cities, life is even more traditional. Morocco has so much beautiful scenery, from mountains and valleys to plains and deserts. With so many films having been made there, there's

a great infrastructure with skilled technicians and workers, and the Moroccan government is always very welcoming to film units. Moroccans are great craftsmen, and we used an enormous number of artisans. They did an amazing job."

The list of international films that have been shot in Morocco since Orson Welles descended upon the coastal city of Essaouira for his *Othello* in 1949 has included the likes of Jerry Bruckheimer's own production of *Black Hawk Down*, directed by Ridley Scott, as well as Scott's *Gladiator, Kingdom of Heaven*, and *Body of Lies*; Alfred Hitchcock's *The Man Who Knew Too Much*; David Lean's *Lawrence of Arabia*; Bernardo Bertolucci's *The Sheltering Sky*; Martin Scorsese's *The Last Temptation of Christ* and *Kundun*; Stephen Sommers's *The Mummy* and *The Mummy Returns*; Oliver Stone's *Alexander*; and enough biblical epics made for both the big and small screens to finance a large chain of kefta restaurants.

Heat and dust, sweat and tears, and a good amount of laughter were all hallmarks of the almost preposterously challenging shoot in the sweltering Moroccan weather. But whether combating temperatures in excess of 120 degrees Fahrenheit, high altitudes, lethal critters in harsh desert landscapes, or the wonderful but often perplexing complexities of a vastly different culture, the company proved to be made of tough stuff. "The most challenging part," notes executive producer Eric McLeod, "are the logistics of moving people around from place to place, not to mention the heat, wild vipers, scorpions, flash floods, and a few other things along the way." And McLeod should know, hav-

ing functioned in the same capacity as "line producer" on *Pirates of the Caribbean: Dead Man's Chest* and *At World's End*, handling the nuts and bolts of daily production throughout their marathon two-year shoot.

The company laid down roots in Marrakesh, a city that seems the definition of *exotic*. Marrakesh has enchanted travelers for centuries with its spectacular, golden, sun-drenched edifices, mosques, minarets, medinas, riads, babs, and kebabs. Every night as the sun descends, the old medina's central square—the Djemaa el Fna—becomes a vision right out of the *Arabian Nights*, with smoke billowing from a hundred outdoor food stalls, Gnawa musicians fervently drumming and singing, acrobats and storytellers performing, vendors selling healing amulets, and medieval-style dentists plying their trade with pliers and small mountains of pulled teeth for all to see.

Two football-field-size warehouses in the Zone Industrielle of Marrakesh were converted into gigantic workshops for the art and wardrobe departments, and months before the cameras rolled, both facilities roiled with tremendous activity. In the art department's warehouse, set decorator Elli Griff, property master David Balfour, and armorer Richard Hooper supervised the creation of thousands of pieces that would adorn the sets and be handled by the actors and stunt players for the duration of the shoot. Their space quickly filled with furniture, pots, statues, weavings, lamps, rugs, wheeled vehicles, and myriad decorations of every variety. Another large complex of offices in the Zone Industrielle was used to house the central production office, including the vast art and visual-effects departments.

For some in the company, both in front of and in back of the cameras, it was a return visit to Morocco. Jerry Bruckheimer produced *Black Hawk Down* further north, in the area of Rabat and Kenitra; first assistant director Simon Warnock and others on his team, including Sallie Hard and Rich Goodwin, had already done Moroccan tours of duty for other films; Jake Gyllenhaal had filmed *Rendition* in the kingdom; Toby Kebbell had shot scenes for *Alexander* there; and Sir Ben Kingsley was a bona fide old Morocco hand. "*Prince of Persia* is my sixth film in Morocco," enthused Sir Ben. "I love the people, their craftsmanship, their ceramics, their architecture, their music, and their graciousness and kindness."

Following six months of active preparation, *Prince of Persia: The Sands of Time* began principal photography on July 23, 2008, in suitably epic fashion, with the first two weeks of filming occurring at an altitude of 8,200 feet in Oukaimden, some seventy-five kilometers above the sizzling-hot city of Marrakesh. Oukaimden was selected as the Hidden Valley location (and ironically would be seen in the final version of the film with a snow-covered mountain range in the background thanks to VFX supervisor Tom Wood). To access this remote location in the High Atlas range, one had to ride through the verdant Ourika Valley and then ascend a winding, less than perfectly built mountain road with perilous drops and switchbacks. Brown

stone and pisé (mud and straw adobe) Berber villages hugged the cliff sides, with colorfully and traditionally attired inhabitants going about their business—much of that having to do with flocks of sheep, goats, and cows, or groves of corn, apples, figs, pears, potatoes, walnuts, and fruit-bearing cacti. Perched above it all was Oukaimden, a ski resort during the winter, with its own hotels and lift. With the skiers being obviously absent in the hot summer sun, the area belonged instead to the Berber shepherds tending to their flocks along the sheer hillsides, using modest stone structures for shelter, just as they have for a millennium.

Supervising location manager Michael Sharp, who currently dwells in the Scottish Highlands but had previously worked in Morocco on both *Alexander* and *Syriana*, made certain that wherever the *Prince of Persia* company went, so would cultural and fiscal responsibility to the local communities. "From location to location, we always employed people from the community," notes Sharp, "so every set has a different group. It's good to know that you haven't just come and used the place. Everyone benefits from the experience, a fair share all around."

It took twenty Moroccan laborers three and a half weeks to build a road into the secluded Hidden Valley location. Meanwhile, location manager Simon Crook and unit manager Kevin Jenkins helped to create the first of many base camps that included a massive catering tent and cooking facilities, and all of the production vehicles from the actors' trailers to tech trucks. An armada of four-wheel-drive Land Rovers was brought in by Morocco transportation coordinator Gerry Gore to ferry the company from the base camp at the foot of the ski lift to the Hidden Valley site—a ride bumpy enough to compete with the Indiana Jones attraction at Disneyland.

On set, producer Jerry Bruckheimer, director Mike Newell, the cast, stunt players, and thousands of attending crew members from all nations—not to mention hundreds of extras and horses—were compelled to imitate the mountain goats herded by the local shepherds, clambering up and down from one cliff side to the next, with less oxygen than usual for a considerable amount of heroic moviemaking action.

Another uncontrollable element in Oukaimden was the fickle weather. "There's a micro climate here at eight thousand two hundred feet," notes Michael Sharp, "so every day, at about three o'clock, the rain and wind hits us." Sure enough, the company grappled with the ferocious North African sun one minute, and then a swift forty-degree temperature drop the next, as the afternoon thunderstorms swept across the mountaintop, forcing everyone to take cover in pop-up tents until they passed.

The weather would, undoubtedly, be the overriding concern during the entire time of filming in Morocco. How could it not? Temperatures in midsummer in North Africa rarely drop below

LEFT: (left to right) Stunt coordinator George Aguilar, technical advisor Harry Humphries, and producer Jerry Bruckheimer on the Alamut set in Tamesloht; RIGHT: Steadicam operator Daniele Massaccesi follows the action with Jake Gyllenhaal and Thomas Dupont in Oukaimden.

100 degrees Fahrenheit, and on most days, the average loomed at about 110–115 degrees Fahrenheit, if not higher. During many days of the shoot, the Moroccan locations were either the hottest places on the face of the earth, or something very close to it.

The extreme heat challenged the company every sweaty step of the way, not just in terms of sheer human endurance, but with regard to practical matters as well. Makeup designer Sallie Jaye and hair designer Jan Archibald had to ensure that their meticulous work, maintained by their talented crews, didn't wither under the punishing sun. Archibald, an Academy Award and BAFTA Award-winner for *La Vie en Rose*, maintained cartloads of wigs and hair appliances, which she used to coif actors and extras in sixth-century styles. Jaye, also a BAFTA Award-winner, somehow had to ensure that the actors wouldn't dissolve into puddles of melted makeup.

After descending to something near sea level—and literally catching their breaths—the company moved to a patch of green next to a bubbling river in Izergane, thirty-eight kilometers southwest of Marrakesh. Here a scene was filmed in a magnificently appointed campaign tent—the Persian army camp outside of Alamut.

Approximately eighteen miles north of Izergane is a flat, dusty, windless stretch of desert called Agafay, where nearly 500 background players portrayed a large chunk of the Persian army, under the command of Nizam (Sir Ben Kingsley), Tus (Richard Coyle), and Garsiv (Toby Kebbell). Prior to the filming of this scene, the film's technical and security advisor, Harry Humphries, and his Moroccan associate Lotfi Saalaoui (a Moroccan police officer assigned to work with the film's security team), had trained the hundreds of local extras, who were previously unschooled in military movement, let alone that of the ancient variety. Humphries, a former Navy SEAL and one of the motion-picture industry's most experienced technical, military, and security advisors, is a longtime associate of Jerry Bruckheimer, and his involvement with the producer has spanned ten films.

"We're trying to turn four hundred people into a marching army within a very short period of time," said Humphries in the middle of a training session held on a large sports field in the Hivernage district of Marrakesh. "Luckily, Sergeant Lotfi is an excellent drill sergeant, so although none of the extras had ever seen a drill field before, he turned them into an excellent marching force in just three days."

On shooting days in and around Marrakesh that required a large number of extras, the production team had set up a superbly organized system humorously called "the sausage factory." A massive, 1,500-meter tent was erected at the Lycée Hassan II, which became a virtual hair, makeup, and wardrobe factory, cooled by huge air conditioners wheezing in the extreme summer heat. An adjoining tent existed just for washing and drying purposes. A large part of the responsibility for getting the background players through the sausage factory fell to costume facilities manager Guven Paternoster, who was a long way from his home in Australia. "When the extras first arrive, they check in, have their breakfast, then wait around until 5:15 a.m. and line up to go through the process. They come into the first part of the sausage factory, the changing area, and come up to the counter where the costumes are held. They all have a number, and the costumers hand them their costume according to that

number." This brilliant system was devised by Kenny Crouch—a man whom costume designer Penny Rose calls "a general in his field." Paternoster continues, "They get changed with the help of costumers, who make sure that they put garments on the right way. Then they check their personal belongings and go into makeup and hair. Then, hopefully, they emerge as a fully dressed extra, and it's into the buses to head to the set. The entire process should last no longer than an hour and a half."

The lunar-like landscape of Bouaissoun, forty-five kilometers northwest of Marrakesh, was perfectly suited for Sheikh Amar's desert kingdom. The scenes involving his gloriously rickety-tickety ostrich racetrack required four days of shooting with the temperamental birds. Following that, the cast and crew moved onto the gigantic Alamut set in the old village of Tamesloht for ten more days of shooting.

Filming in Tamesloht, which was literally within an existing community, required some delicate negotiations between the company and the village leaders. "The Alamut set was constructed within the walls of the original kasbah, which in historic times was the final kasbah before Marrakesh," informs Michael Sharp. "There are six hundred families in Tamesloht, and, as with the other locations, we've rotated local workers so that everyone in the village gets their fair share."

Everyone on the *Prince of Persia* production team worked to ensure that filming would cause as little disruption to the daily routine of the village as possible. Each day's call sheet carried the following request: EXISTING VILLAGE COMMUNITY. PLEASE WORK RESPECTFULLY. VEHICLES MUST NOT DRIVE ONTO THIS SET.

ABOVE: Moroccan police officer Lotfi Saalaoui (with bullhorn) and security advisor Lachen Bouhaddi drill Moroccan background players in the art of becoming an ancient Persian army; LEFT: Executive producer Mike Stenson of Jerry Bruckheimer Films and Jake Gyllenhaal on the final day of filming in Morocco in the Merzouga sand dunes; RIGHT: The remarkable Nasaf set constructed adjacent to Kasbah Ait Ben Haddou near Ouarzazate.

Working side by side with the local community was no problem. Dealing with the extreme heat, dust, and stagnant air at Tamesloht was something else again. "Walking onto the Alamut set is one of those magic moments," says Daud Shah, who portrays the Alamutian warrior Asoka. "You have thousands of people, hundreds of extras, and every costume is totally unique and different. You walk in there and are instantly transported to a mythical city, which exists beyond the borders of Persia, towards Afghanistan, Pakistan, and India. But the sun is baking hot, and there's dust everywhere. Your lungs fill with dirt when the horses gallop by. It's been so hot that some of the stunt guys' cigarette lighters have exploded. But the armor I wear for the role has helped me shed a few pounds."

Ten days later, it was time for the *Prince of Persia* gypsy corps to pack their bags and hit the road for the 200-kilometer, two-and-a-half-hour drive through the 7,415-foot-Tizi n'Tichka pass in the High Atlas range. They journeyed southeast to Ouarzazate, the realistically self-proclaimed "Hollywood of North Africa," also known as "The Door to the Desert." The capital of southern Morocco, Ouarzazate sits astride the Draa River at the end of the Tichka Road and is dominated by an Atlas range that looms to the north of the small city.

The dun-colored, modestly proportioned city had, over the years, housed an enormous number of international productions since the *Lawrence of Arabia* company pitched its tents there (in a time before luxury hotels) in 1961. Thus, Jerry Bruckheimer and his *Prince of Persia* team were literally following in the footsteps of David Lean, and dozens of other directors since,

who fell in love with the dramatic landscapes and kasbahs surrounding Ouarzazate. There are now two full-size film studios in Ouarzazate: CLA (where the *Prince of Persia* production facilities would be based) and Atlas, where the walls of Jerusalem were built for Ridley Scott's *Kingdom of Heaven*. Gigantic statuary constructed for the television version of *The Ten Commandments* can still be seen from the main road.

The call sheet of the first day of filming at the Little Fint Oasis, forty minutes outside of Ouarzazate, held two warnings, one more terrifying than the other:

PLEASE DO NOT TOUCH THE OSTRICH ON SET TODAY

and, even worse:

BEWARE – SNAKES & SCORPIONS CAN BE FOUND AT THIS LOCATION UNDER AND AROUND THE ROCKS. BE CAUTIOUS.

"Ostriches I can deal with," mumbled an unnerved on-set hair stylist. "Snakes and scorpions, though, freak me out!"

There was nothing to fear, however, because "Snake Dude" (as his position was very loudly announced on his T-shirt) was on the case. This was a Moroccan gentleman, always smiling, greatly experienced in the ways of vipers and venomous beasties, whose task was to clear the shooting areas of the deadly pests before the cast and crew arrived, and during the shooting days. It didn't take long for Snake Dude's glass jars to become filled with the pernicious creatures, all of which were released at the end of the workdays.

The following two days, though, brought near catastrophe

SO I DREW

I'm not a trained artist, but I love to draw. For me it's less about the result than the act itself. Drawing takes me out of the "thinking" mode of writing screenplays and designing video games, and focuses me on what's in front of me in a way that's deeply restful.

I felt a bit self-conscious bringing a sketchbook to the *Prince of Persia* set. I wasn't sure I was ready to go public with my private hobby. I'm glad I did.

Since childhood, I'd absorbed the mystique of *One Thousand and One Nights* through Hollywood movies—from *Thief of Bagdad* to *Lawrence of Arabia* to *Raiders of the Lost Ark*. Those movies filled my head (and their soundtracks played on my stereo) twenty years ago, as I tinkered with assembly-language code to make a Persian prince run, jump, and climb across the Apple II computer screen to save a kingdom from a scheming vizier.

THE DIRECTOR'S TENT INVADED BY MONGOLS ON THEIR LUNCH BREAK

That prince was forty pixels high. His soundtrack was beeps and buzzes. But to me, he was an action hero in the cinematic tradition of Douglas Fairbanks, Errol Flynn, and Harrison Ford.

Two decades later, I found myself in the Moroccan desert, staring at the *Prince of Persia* logo stenciled on the black canvas of directors chairs. The chairs bore names I'd esteemed even in my Apple II days, names to conjure with: John Seale, Sir Ben Kingsley, Mike Newell, Jerry Bruckheimer. The prince's journey had come full circle.

Being on the *Prince of Persia* set was a powerful experience for me. Sketching gave me a way to channel my impressions and emotions, and time to absorb it all. It reconnected me to my childhood self, to the kid who liked to draw and was enthralled by *One Thousand and One Nights*.

Jake & Gemma waiting for next take

Sometimes, when I stopped to reflect on the journey, a big goofy smile would spread across my face. I didn't want Newell to catch me wearing that expression, because he'd give me a scowl: What are you grinning about?

So I drew.

—Jordan Mechner

to the company, as high winds kicked up classic, full-on, ferocious sandstorms before the rain came, tamping down the blinding grains of earth but drenching the company and its equipment. All in all, it was ironically appropriate for a film entitled *Prince of Persia: The Sands of Time.* "When we first scouted in Morocco," recalls Mike Newell, "there was a fifty-mile-per-hour wind blowing, but the locals would not dignify it with the name *sandstorm.* They said, 'This isn't a sandstorm, just a little breeze.' A sandstorm is a hell of a terrifying thing, because everything goes black, you can't see a thing, and it chokes you. And one of the great scenes in the movie takes place in a sandstorm."

Constant maintenance of equipment in such extreme weather conditions would bedevil Australian director of photography John Seale and his camera crew throughout filming in Morocco, but he had already experienced similar conditions shooting in Tunisia on *The English Patient,* for which he won an Academy Award. "We were able to acclimatize to this heat, and the cameras were equipped for it," notes Seale, "but even so, we had a continual fogging of the negative. Its origin eluded us for weeks, but eventually we had to agree that it was the incredible heat that was fogging the film. Nothing we did could get rid of it. A lot of preparation went into the equipment. The dust storms and sand dervishes wreaked havoc with sand

OPPOSITE: A selection of Jordan Mechner's sketches done while on set in Morocco. BELOW: Mike Newell, director of photography John Seale (in white cap), and the camera crew prepare to film Jake Gyllenhaal and Gemma Arterton on horseback in the blazing hot Tinrheras Plains near Erfoud.

in the cameras, which can cause scratches and, consequently, reshoots, so the camera crew was particularly careful. A lot of the locations were logistical nightmares, with one access in and one out, and because we were shooting with multiple cameras, there was nowhere to hide the base camps, so it put a large burden on all departments.

"I do love the desert," continues Seale, "as I do the outback in Australia, and the locations in Morocco were sensational. Every day was an adventure, and we moved all the time, so there was never a chance to get bored with one place. If you didn't like it, just wait for the next one! One of the nicest locations was the Little Fint Oasis outside of Ouarzazate, which I believe is a favorite of the king of Morocco. We later rebuilt it on a soundstage at Pinewood for a night shoot. It was a lovely area and a quiet spot deep in the desert."

Indeed, the so-called Little and Big Fint were picture-perfect oases right out of Orientalist paintings, or Hollywood dreams. The sudden rush of greenery in the middle of such endless brown expanses was a miraculous sight. One of the company enjoying the surroundings was Jordan Mechner. The soft-spoken creator of the original Prince of Persia video game had flown in from his Los Angeles home to spend some time observing how his baby was making the journey to the big screen. "It's one thing to have done Prince of Persia as a video game for the past twenty years," marveled Mechner, "and it's another thing to actually be in a desert with real weather, real camels, real horses. Jerry and Mike and everybody involved have worked so hard to make this as real as possible." For his own amusement, and perhaps posterity, everywhere Mechner went his little black sketchbook

went with him, and it became a common sight to see him sitting unobtrusively on a rock or beneath a date palm, quietly creating delightful artistic images of what he beheld, with notes capturing his thoughts, snippets of dialogues, and moments in time.

The next location for *Prince of Persia: The Sands of Time* was truly special. Named a UNESCO World Heritage Site in 1987, the towering ancient ksar (fortified city) of Ait Ben Haddou was built with brown pisé (earth and rubble) tighremt (granary) structures designed with Berber motifs. Adjacent to the ksar was a perfect place for Wolf Kroeger to build the magnificent Nasaf marketplace, incorporating elements of Ait Ben Haddou in the background. In normal conditions, one accesses Ait Ben Haddou by parking on the far side of the Oued Mellah, usually a bone-dry riverbed studded with stones.

But fate had something else in store for the *Prince of Persia* company, as an unseasonal series of rainstorms turned the Oued Mellah into something resembling a real river—which threatened to strand the company. "We were three days away from filming," recalls executive producer Eric McLeod, "and all of a sudden, heavy rains up in the mountains about fifty miles away washed out the road that got us to the location." Michael Sharp noted, "Local people in their eighties have said that they've never experienced this kind of rain during the summer. We had to call in machinery that filled the river with rock so we could at least cross in four-by-four vehicles."

This was but one of the myriad and sometimes surreal challenges facing Morocco transportation coordinator Gerry Gore, a plainspoken man with much North African experience behind him on such films as *Gladiator* and *Sahara*. "Ait Ben Haddou was the most difficult location we had in terms of logistics, because of the rain situation," says Gore. "Unfortunately, if you got rain thirty or forty kilometers away from Ait Ben Haddou, the river would begin rising. It rose to four feet of water, so we couldn't cross until it went down again. The problem was that if during the shooting day the river rose again, we wouldn't be able to get out of there and back to Ouarzazate." The solution was to utilize an old existing road that avoided the river altogether but took at least twenty minutes longer to access Ait Ben Haddou.

At nearly the same moment the company began filming at Ait Ben Haddou, on September 2, 2008, the holy month of Ramadan commenced, a sacred time for the Moroccans who made up the better part of the crew, stunt team, and background players. According to the laws of Islam, Muslims must fast from sunrise to sunset for thirty days. For Muslims, this is a holy time of prayer, self-reflection, and purification, in which they learn compassion and appreciation for life's goodness. However, the extraordinary Moroccan crew and cast members were unflagging in their devotion to the company and the task at hand. They continued shooting for ten to twelve hours a day in increasingly intense heat, while at the same time observing the tenets of their faith. The call sheets posted during every day of Ramadan made the production's philosophy clear: RAMADAN–PLEASE BE RESPECTFUL OF YOUR FELLOW CREW MEMBERS WHO ARE FASTING. Some non-Muslim crew members actually fasted to show solidarity with their Moroccan colleagues, enjoying *iftar* (the breaking of the fast) together at sunset with a traditional meal of figs and *harira* (lentil, vegetable, and meat soup).

While filming in Ouarzazate, both the first and second units also shot within the extraordinary pisé walls of the Kasbah Taourirte, an ancient dwelling right in the center of town. In fact, the kasbah was once all that existed of Ouarzazate, before the French overlords built their new garrison town around it, and it still has a beautiful and primitive atmosphere exuding strength and exoticism in equal measure. It's still the beating heart of Ouarzazate, its narrow alleyways teeming with residents coming and going, playing cards or dominoes, buying, selling, and haggling in tiny shops.

After filming in the dramatic Tiwiyne Gorge, which resembled the landscapes of the American Southwest, the company packed up and drove 322 kilometers due east along the "Route of a Thousand Kasbahs" to Erfoud. At a veritable stone's throw from the Algerian border, the filmmakers selected a suitably desolate stretch of desert to serve as the forbidding entrance to the Valley of the Slaves, where Sheikh Amar and his raggedy bandits hold sway.

The final two days of filming in Morocco took place among the famed Merzouga sand dunes, mountains of sand rising like a golden-hued mirage to heights of 450 feet from a black, rocky, unforgiving plain. "I think it's really appropriate that a movie titled *Prince of Persia: The Sands of Time* ends its Morocco shoot in sand dunes," said executive producer Eric McLeod. "It's a wonderful irony." These are the classic dunes of every *Arabian Nights* fantasy, sculpted, shaped, and rippled by the hot winds, their colors changing with the movement of the sun. On the final day in Morocco, Friday, September 12, 2008, the thermometer almost blew its mercury at a mind-and-body-numbing 125 degrees Fahrenheit. Crew members from the Western Hemisphere wrapped themselves in indigo Tuareg head coverings and went shoeless, to make walking easier among the deep dunes. The Moroccan crew members looked at these now swarthy, sweat-soaked, sunbaked visitors from afar with a mixture of bemusement and affection. After more than two months, the foreigners had started to look just like them!

According to facilities manager Gregoire Mouveau, the company consumed 1,114,894 bottles of water to keep themselves properly hydrated during their time in Morocco. That comes to approximately 597,704 liters of water. "We had a full-size first-unit crew, a full-size second crew, an aerial crew, more than three hundred drivers getting people from one place to another, upwards of seven hundred extras, and days in which the caterers had to serve more than seventeen hundred meals," explains Eric McLeod. "We had five hundred international crew members, plus almost fifteen hundred Moroccans working at any one time. It's been a pretty massive undertaking."

"My DNA now has the Moroccan desert in it, because I've definitely breathed in my share of sand," laughed Jake Gyllenhaal, reflecting on the experience. "I grew up in Southern California, and the weather and topography of Morocco are actually

quite similar, so it wasn't too rough for me. I had shot here before, but I'd never actually gone as far into the desert and seen as much of Morocco as I did on *Prince of Persia*. It's a really beautiful country. There were times, on off days, when I'd just drive and drive, just amazed at the landscapes and the culture. Moroccan people are the sweetest, kindest people, and the hardest workers. I'm really going to miss them a lot. I just think Moroccans are wonderful people."

"It was hot, hot, hot," recalled Gemma Arterton after returning to England, "and the dust was everywhere. There was one scene in which Dastan, Sheikh Amar, and the Sheikh's men gallop up to me on horseback, and with the amount of dust that kicked up, I was literally covered in it . . . but it was quite funny, and a great experience to be out there. It was extreme, but it was really satisfying to think that we had gotten through it all. It was beautiful as well, because Morocco has such varied landscapes. One minute you're in the desert, and the next you're in the mountains looking at snow. It's just incredible."

"The English are supposed to have this special thing for the desert, because England is so small, green, and wet," notes Mike Newell, "and the English can breathe free when they get into vast, dry spaces. And it's true. The desert is a very beautiful and mysterious place to be."

For the final shot in Morocco, Mike Newell directed eight-year-old Daisy Doidge-Hill, a charming little British actress portraying the first guardian of the Dagger of Time in flashback scenes. The shoot ended just as the fiery sun was descending over the Merzouga dunes, turning the sand magnificent, kaleido-scopic shades of brown, ocher, and gold. First assistant director Simon Warnock—a veteran of large-scale moviemaking with such epics behind him as the Lord of the Rings trilogy, Oliver Stone's *Alexander*, and Baz Luhrmann's *Australia*—called the last of forty "wraps" in Morocco. Cast and crew made their way across the dunes to base camp as the sun descended and a huge oval moon rose brightly above an ever-darkening blue sky. The sands had become a fiery orange, and the Moroccan crew members enjoyed breaking the Ramadan fast with their *iftar* meal of *harira* and dates. The beauty of the landscape, both natural and human, was transcendent.

That final night in Erfoud, with a charter jet due to arrive the next morning to ferry the company to London, vigorous drums and music permeated the air at the crew hotel as a Berber ensemble played. An adorable eleven-month-old camel named Mounis—that looked like a cartoon character, with his ever-smiling face and long eyelashes—made the rounds being petted and having photos taken with the crew. A billion stars flickered far above in the otherwise ink-black sky, and the magic of Morocco and the desert truly dawned on the cast and crew members just before they were to depart for the more cosmopolitan climes of London. Many of them, however much they might have suffered the extremes of the climate and topography, realized what would be lost in returning to England. They would be leaving a place in which mystery and magic still hold sway for a brilliant Western metropolis in which one can find absolutely everything—except what's intrinsic in the Moroccan desert and in the ancient peoples who inhabit it.

JOHN SEALE: PAINTING ON FILM

Johnohn Seale is a painter, a master of cinematography," says Jerry Bruckheimer of the Academy Award-winning director of photography selected to illuminate the world depicted in *Prince of Persia: The Sands of Time*. Indeed, the veteran Australian cinematographer has been painting with light on film for more than twenty years, his artistry shown to best advantage in such films as Peter Weir's *Witness*, *The Mosquito Coast*, and *Dead Poets Society*; George Miller's *Lorenzo's Oil*; Wolfgang Petersen's *The Perfect Storm*; Anthony Minghella's *The English Patient* (for which Seale won both the Oscar and a BAFTA Award), *The Talented Mr. Ripley*, and *Cold Mountain*; and Chris Columbus's *Harry Potter and the Sorcerer's Stone*.

"John Seale and Wolf Kroeger are the two people who have the most to do with the look of the film, and it's a magnificent looking beast," says Mike Newell. "John and I had enormous talks about color and lighting, whether it would be harsh or soft, about back light and front light, which way the camera would move, and so on. We carefully worked out a camera language for the movie, and it looks absolutely wonderful because of John, who's very, very savvy and has an enormous amount of experience."

"*Prince of Persia: The Sands of Time* was a very interesting film to approach," says Seale. "On the one hand, it is set in a period that can only be researched by paintings, scrolls, statues, and hieroglyphics . . . and on the other, we were to make a movie of action, adventure, and romance. To be able to combine these aspects, to set the film in its period and satisfy the audience's needs, was most challenging. So the approach was one of a beautiful time and place, with overtones of menace. It would be the combination of beautiful light and surroundings, with the intrusion of darker, colder light with the Hassansins, to the end, with a kaleidoscope of color emanating from the Sandglass of the Gods."

As were Jerry Bruckheimer, Mike Newell, and production designer Wolf Kroeger, John Seale was also influenced by nineteenth-century Orientalist paintings. Explains Seale, "The study of these artists had a great influence on the overall photography. The Orientalists had this ability to accentuate their subject matter by painting the details they wished to emphasize and then letting the rest fall away into dark corners or storm-laden skies. And so, to be able to take the audience's eye to where we wanted it, we borrowed a bit of that in the initial lighting. We let backgrounds fall away, and we also composed the frame to honor the painters. The Orientalists' attention to light and detail were also a major part of the cinematography. The Orientalists made use of a great array of color, or lack of it, to once again bring your eye to the area of the subject they wished you to concentrate on."

Seale decided from the start that he would make great use of DI, which is short for digital intermediate. This is a relatively new, high-tech process of digitalizing a motion picture and manipulating color and other image characteristics to change and enhance the film's look, allowing for infinitely detailed and sometimes remarkably subtle changes to color and composition. For a painter like John Seale, it's another tool in the toolbox, but an important one. "What might not have been achieved in camera can be enhanced later in the DI stage," notes Seale, "so we'll be able to embellish the visual emotion, particularly after the editing. Once the final cut has been locked, then we can start to embellish the look of the film as an overall presentation.

"*Prince of Persia: The Sands of Time* will utilize DI to its fullest," continues Seale. "To be able to smooth the film will not be enough. We will be adding changes in color, density, and composition to enhance the movie for the total enjoyment of the audience. It is a smorgasbord of images that will help drive the action and emotion throughout and remain true to the essence of the script. The DI is a fantastic tool for this kind of film. There are some movies which do not need a heavy input of DI, but *Prince of Persia* will have a good bit of enhancing to keep the feeling of the era and period and also satisfy the action, romance, and drama."

A World Within

The sudden transition from ruthlessly hot and routinely chaotic Morocco to the staid, cool, controlled confines of historic Pinewood Studios was a kind of culture shock for the company, even for the prodigious number of Brits in the cast and on the crew. Having become acclimatized (for the most part) to working amid the stunning natural environments of mountains, canyons, and sand dunes, the cast and crew had to make some quick adjustments. The fully fabricated but no less wondrous sets designed by Wolf Kroeger were constructed on nine soundstages of the historic studio in the bucolic burg of Iver Heath in Buckinghamshire, England.

"We filmed some of *King Arthur* and *National Treasure: Book of Secrets* at Pinewood," said Jerry Bruckheimer, "and it was good to return. Morocco was amazing, but shooting in the UK gave the entire company a chance to settle into a comfortable pattern that didn't include sandstorms and scorpions."

"Well, at least the rocks and stones *look* real," noted Jake Gyllenhaal of the first interior setting to be shot at Pinewood, in mid-September 2008, an elaborate cave complete with waterfalls and pools. "But, yeah, it's strange to be in such different circumstances. There's nothing better than being in a real environment, being in a place where you feel like you go back centuries. We all live in such modernized times, and when you come to Pinewood you're being driven through a huge metropolis. When we were filming in Morocco, we were all in the middle of the desert, dirty and dusty. I can't recall the amount of times between takes you had to just get the sand out of your eyes, mouth, and ears so you looked like you weren't literally made of sand. The realism of it all was indelible. But here, onstage in London, we can mix reality with fantasy, which is all the more interesting to watch."

"The sets at Pinewood were awesome," enthused cinematographer John Seale. "Wolf Kroeger and set decorator Elli Griff once again excelled in design, construction, and dressing of the massive sets. It was a long way from the heat and dust of Morocco, but the sets they constructed and dressed made you feel you were right there. In the final version of the film, actors will exit a door at Pinewood and come out in Morocco, and it will look seamless, thanks to the art department, which was always on top of all the problems. The large sets were a challenge to light, particularly the 007 Stage, but our gaffers, Mo Flam and Steve Costello, were magicians. They kept well ahead of us and had all the stages ready to go as we got to them. They had a great crew of good, hardworking men, and it's a credit to them. The Italian grips, under Tommaso Mele, were the same. I had worked with them on three other films, and they were fantastic. Nothing was too hard, as long as they found a good Italian restaurant!"

Pinewood Studios is like a living museum of British filmmaking history, having housed one classic after another since opening in 1936. Twenty James Bond films have been shot at Pinewood, from the first entry in that durable series, *Dr. No*, all the way to the most recent, *Quantum of Solace*. In fact, the famous Albert R. Broccoli 007 Stage, with its massive dimensions of 374 feet in length, 158 feet in width and forty-one to fifty feet in height—the biggest stage in Europe, at around 59,000 square feet—would be one of the most important of the Pinewood stages utilized for *Prince of Persia: The Sands of Time*. Coincidentally, it was producer and publicity executive Saul Cooper—the father of *Prince of Persia* unit photographer Andrew Cooper—who organized the christening ceremony for the stage in 1976, when it was constructed for the filming of *The Spy Who Loved Me*.

With the exception of Heatherden Hall, the gracious old Victorian manor housing the corporate offices and the wood-paneled restaurant, Pinewood is not what one would call glamorous. There's an atmospheric patina of industrial grit overhanging the facility, and if it feels something like a Dickensian factory, perhaps that's appropriate—it's a factory built for the creation of that curiously dreamlike medium called motion pictures.

At Pinewood, the company settled into a routine utterly different from what they had experienced in Morocco. It was more predictable, more controllable, and certainly cooler. "It's as if you're running a long race, and Morocco was the uphill part," says executive producer Patrick McCormick. "Now we're on a nice, level path. We can walk from one location to the next just by going from one soundstage to another, and we don't have weather to contend with. And instead of catering an average of seven hundred people a day, we're down to just two-fifty or three hundred. In Morocco we had three hundred drivers alone!"

As the company filmed inside the dry, if sometimes chilly, soundstages, even the blustery, rainy British weather held little sway. Battling traffic on the M4 or A40 from London to Iver Heath was pretty much the toughest challenge facing the crew—although, for the non-English crew members, it was often difficult to identify the ingredients of the British dishes in the lunch tent. Shepherd's pie and cottage pie, bangers and mash, bubble and squeak, toad-in-the-hole, and other whimsically named victuals dominated the menu. For *pudding*—which is the British term for "dessert" (whether it's an actual pudding or not)—various sweet concoctions were summarily drowned in delicious, fresh-from-the-farm, artery-hardening cream or custard. Sadly, the pudding amusingly known as Spotted Dick was never on the menu.

Standing on the ornate Nasaf throne-room set on S Stage, a tall, wiry, unpretentiously attired gentleman looked around and mused, "This reminds me so much of the buildings where we filmed in Damascus on *Lawrence of Arabia*." It's a casual reference that would make any film buff's jaw drop to the floor, but then again, this was Michael Stevenson talking, a man who knows what an epic film really is. Having devoted more than fifty years to the British film industry as an assistant director, Stevenson could be called a living national treasure of the U.K.

On *Prince of Persia: The Sands of Time*, Stevenson honored the production with four days of work, nimbly handling vast throngs of background players for the huge Alamut Palace banquet scene, politely but firmly putting them in position as per Mike Newell's commands. A typical Michael Stevenson request might be "Would the lovely background players please step this way toward the makeup tent?" as befits the consummate gentleman he is (although heaven protect the disobedient under his watch). The astonishing list of films on which Michael Stevenson has worked following *Lawrence*, has included such elephantine spectacles as *The Fall of the Roman Empire*, *Doctor Zhivago*, *Ryan's Daughter*, *Lord Jim*, *The Charge of the Light Brigade*, *Alexander*, and Jerry Bruckheimer's production of *Pearl Harbor*. He also worked for Stanley Kubrick on the filmmaker's *Barry Lyndon*, *The Shining*, and *Full Metal Jacket*. Having worked with and for some of the biggest names in world cinema, Stevenson affirmed, "I would put Jerry Bruckheimer in the same category as Sam Spiegel, Dino De Laurentiis, and Samuel Bronston. Even above their category, because Mr. Bruckheimer has not only been more successful with his feature films, but in television as well."

And when his week of work on *Prince of Persia* came to an end, Stevenson did exactly what he's been doing for more than half a century: he almost immediately found his next job, serving as first assistant director on Neil Jordan's *Ondine*. For this living legend, retirement is not an option!

On the final day of shooting—the 105th, to be exact, on what turned out to be a very happy and celebratory Friday the thirteenth (of December 2008)—it was a classic British winter day: chilly, dreary, windy, and, in the local vernacular, pissing down rain. In the course of that one day, the company was filming on no fewer than six separate soundstages, with Mike Newell and the rest of the company shifting back and forth at Mach speed, hurrying to finish "bits and bobs" of sequences with Jake Gyllenhaal and Gemma Arterton. Finally, at 7:30 p.m. on the Avrat rooftops set, Mike Newell called, "Cut!" for the final time.

"All right," Newell concluded with a wide smile. "Where's the damn champagne?" Corks popped, and crew members embraced, swore eternal friendship, and discussed what they'd do with their time now that their Persian adventure had come to an expected but nonetheless poignant end.

"The idea that films spring fully formed from your own forehead is complete nonsense," says Newell. "As a director, you rely on a huge number of people, and everyone made their own huge contributions to *Prince of Persia*."

RIGHT: Legendary British assistant director Michael Stevenson on the Nasaf Throne Room set at Pinewood Studios.

For most of the *Prince of Persia: The Sands of Time* company, it was over. But for Jerry Bruckheimer and Mike Newell, there was still a seventeen-month postproduction period ahead, which promised to be nearly as challenging and intense as the five months of filming. In putting the finishing touches on the film, Bruckheimer and Newell would rely on associate producer Pat Sandston, the postproduction maestro of Jerry Bruckheimer Films; JBF postproduction supervisor Tami Goldman and an army of film editors, sound editors, ADR and sound-effects artists; cinematographer John Seale; Tom Wood and his visual-effects crew; and composer Harry Gregson-Williams.

Tackling the considerable accumulation of film were three of the best editors in the business: the legendary Michael Kahn, a seven-time Academy Award nominee who won the statue for Steven Spielberg's *Raiders of the Lost Ark, Schindler's List*, and *Saving Private Ryan* (Kahn has edited twenty films directed by Spielberg since *Close Encounters of the Third Kind* in 1977 and numerous others produced by the filmmaker); Martin Walsh, who won an Oscar for Rob Marshall's *Chicago*; and Mick Audsley, who previously collaborated with Newell on such films as *Harry Potter and the Goblet of Fire* and *Mona Lisa Smile*.

The cast and behind-the-scenes talents, of course, went on to new projects. Jerry Bruckheimer, juggling eight television shows in production and two pilots about to go in front of the cameras, began shooting *The Sorcerer's Apprentice* in New York City. He was also developing a shipload of feature films, among them *The Lone Ranger* and the fourth entry in the Pirates of the Caribbean juggernaut, both of which would reunite the producer with Johnny Depp.

Mike Newell announced that he would direct a film of John Masefield's 1930 children's classic *The Box of Delights*.

Life went on for one and all, and only a time rewind could bring them together again.

But *Prince of Persia: The Sands of Time* is the sum of the company's talents and dedication, and, at least on this massive, unforgettable project, the cast and crew made their own destinies.

AFTERWORD BY

Jake Gyllenhaal

A legendary producer; a wonderful director; a video game legacy; all the toys, magic, and skills that Hollywood has at its command; and the chance to bring life to a classic character who is blessed with crazy fighting skills and who's practically unbound by gravity—who wouldn't be excited?! I had the help of gymnasts, swordsmen, veteran stuntmen, and the inventor of parkour himself, David Belle, all of whom served as guides throughout this fantastical journey. And to think—before I started shooting *Prince of Persia*, I had never really been in an action movie, despite having dreamed about doing one since I was a kid.

So I thought I would share a little of what it was like to do my first stunt: a massive, death-defying, thirty-five-foot jump. It was quite an experience, a day I'll never forget. . . .

Our legendary, red-haired, six-foot-eight-inch stunt coordinator, Greg Powell, cigar wedged between his teeth, greeted me when I pulled up to the set in Ouarzazate, Morocco—the gate to the Sahara. He had a great big smile on his face as he threw

out his hand for a shake. Pointing to the top of a kasbah, he said, "Follow me mate, we're goin' to the top." On the roof there was a rig fitted with a pulley system that would be attached to the harness I was wearing. The rig was designed to ease my fall through the air as I jumped off the top of one kasbah and landed on the roof of the other, thirty-five feet below. It had taken me about twenty minutes to get the harness on under my already elaborate costume, and the harness fit so tightly that my gait was more like Frankenstein's monster than that of a Persian prince. But the good news was, I didn't have to walk in the scene, I only had to jump.

I waddled up the dark stairs of the ancient building and out on to its rooftop, where my stunt double, Mark Fichera, was waiting. It was 115 degrees, sun blazing. Mark is a man of few words. He greeted me with a nod, pointed to the edge of the rooftop and said, "We're gonna hook you up to the rig and then you're gonna jump off." He walked me slowly to the edge and we looked down to the neighboring roof, thirty-five feet below.

My head spun just a little. "Kinda high," I said. "Yeah," he said, "but we'll make sure you're safe." He half grinned, shrugged his shoulders, and then gave me a quick, hard pat on the back. Mark had done the jump earlier in the day so I asked him how it felt. "It's high," he said. Great.

We stepped back from the edge and the rigging guys hooked a wire to my back. Truth be told, I was a little freaked, but I decided to put my trust in these men. They're the best in the business and sometimes you just have to admit how little you know, trust the guys that do, and go for it.

They made sure that I was secure, let me look over the edge a few times to see where I was supposed to land, and then headed back inside so they wouldn't be seen in the shot. And I was left standing there alone. I took a few deep breaths. This is what I had dreamed of doing since I was a kid. I couldn't believe it. I jumped around a bit to shake off any excess nerves and before I could even think, I heard, "We're rolling!" I focused on the edge. "Three . . . two . . . one!" I started to run. I couldn't believe this was happening. " . . . Action!!!!" And with crazy, wild abandon I jumped!

By the time my head met up with my body I had landed, unknowingly perfectly, and the crew applauded. I looked up. Mark put his hand out and gave me a big thumbs-up. That was it. All I had to do was trust. First big jump done. The first of many.

Jumping from rooftop to rooftop, running up walls, and fighting Alamutians wouldn't have been possible alone. Simon Waterson, Ben Cooke, George Aguilar, Greg Powell, Tom Dupont, Mark Fichera, and David Belle were all there with me. They were the men that helped me create Dastan, the warrior. Each contributed a key element: Mr. Waterson challenged me with daily 5 a.m. pre-shoot workouts ("Up and at 'em mate! Sun's almost up! Bit o' cardio and weights before we head off to set!"); Mr. Aguilar and Mr. Powell (two of the best stunt coordinators in the business) gave me daily run-downs of the plan for the day's action; and Mr. Cooke, Mr. Fichera, Mr. Dupont, and Mr. Belle actually did the stunts with me, walking me through each sequence, step by step, jump by jump, sword slash by sword slash. Equally, and each in their own right, they are all Dastan. Who knew that it could take eight men to create one character?

That day pretty much encapsulates my entire *Prince of Persia* experience. Every day, every single cast and crew member came together and we all leapt into the unknown. The efforts of thousands of people on three continents speaking half a dozen languages went into the making of this movie. I hope that this book has shown you a bit of their work, because the goal of the film's contributors, my seven other Dastans included, is to remain invisible. I am hopeful that you enjoy *Prince of Persia* and that you appreciate how many millions of hours of work were put into it by thousands of wonderful people.

ACKNOWLEDGMENTS

I've attempted in this book to tell a story of the collective work of more than a thousand people around the world, who themselves were a microcosm of everything I've always loved about moviemaking: individuals from diverse cultures and backgrounds, speaking an array of languages, somehow merging their talents—whether operating cameras, cobbling sandals, or driving four-wheel-drive vehicles through the desert—toward the same goal. So to the entire cast and crew of *Prince of Persia: The Sands of Time*, wherever they may be, thank you, *shukran, merci, grazie, gracias, danke, takk, koszonom, dakujem,* etc. All of my gratitude to Jerry Bruckheimer for his endless inspiration and generosity, and to my friends and colleagues at Jerry Bruckheimer Films, including Mike Stenson, Chad Oman, Melissa Reid, Pat Sandston, Tami Goldman, and Jill Weiss. Many thanks to Mike Newell for providing me with a daily feast of jaw-dropping filmmaking in both Morocco and at Pinewood Studios, which could have given me enough material for a volume three times the size of this one. Appreciation and respect to Jordan Mechner, not only for his wonderful contributions to this book, but for giving all of us a job by creating Prince of Persia in the first place! And a deep bow of gratitude to Jake Gyllenhaal, not only for embodying the prince himself, but also for contributing a marvelous Afterword to this book. Thank you to everyone at Walt Disney Studios, particularly Oren Aviv, Jason Reed, Ryan Stankevich, Christine Cadena, Erik Schmudde and, especially, Jon Rogers. A big shout-out to the great staff at Herzog Productions, including Mark Herzog, Jack Kney, Joy Lissandrello, Brandon Carroll, Sara O'Reilly, and Ed Farmer. At Disney Editions, my gratitude to a marvelous editor, Jessica Ward, for her expert guidance, as well as to Wendy Lefkon, Jennifer Eastwood, and Jill Rapaport, and to the book's producer, Clark Wakabayashi, and the designers Christopher Measom and Timothy Shaner. Appreciation to Jody Revenson for her invaluable contributions to this book in its early stages. A very special bravo and thank you to my friend Andrew Cooper, the brilliant unit photographer of *Prince of Persia: The Sands of Time*, an artist of the first rank whose magnificent imagery adorns this volume.

This book can only be dedicated to my wife, Yuko, and our daughters, Miyako and Kimiko. How or why on earth they put up with my marathon absences while I'm working on far-flung locations, I may never know. But the truth is, with them, I never have to ask that question. It has something to do with love.

—Michael Singer